ASTRONAUTICS VS. FANTASIA

"The lenger life, I wote, the greater sin;
The greater sin, the greater punishment:
All those great battels, whitch thou boasts to win
Through strife, and blood-shed, and avengement,
Now prayed, hereafter deare thou shalt repent;
For life must life, and blood must blood, repay.
Is not enough thy evill life forespent?
For he that once hath missed the right way,
The further he doth goe, the further he doth stray."

SPENSER (*The Faerie Queene*)
Book I, Canto IX.

The
Enchanted Planet

by
Pierre Barbet

Translated by
C. J. Richards

DAW BOOKS, INC.
DONALD A. WOLLHEIM, PUBLISHER

1301 Avenue of the Americas
New York, N. Y.　　　10019

COPYRIGHT © 1975 BY DAW BOOKS, INC.

Original edition entitled *La Planète Enchantée,* copyright ©, 1973, by Editions Fleuve Noir, Paris, France. Published by arrangement with Editions Fleuve Noir.

Translation by C. J. Richards.

All Rights Reserved.

Cover art by Michael Whelan.

FIRST PRINTING, JULY 1975

1 2 3 4 5 6 7 8 9

PRINTED IN U.S.A.

Introduction

Commander Pentoser cried out in astonishment, "Focus the screen! Something is coming towards us. Is that a wreck or a spaceship?"

Captain Setni leaped from his chair to glance at the spaceship's radar. With a sigh of relief, he announced: "There's no doubt that it's a wreck floating in space. Plot its coordinates and contact President Kalapol."

Pentoser, using the radio transmitter called: "Spaceship *Zineb* from Pollux, patrolling the Corona Borealis sector. We are reporting an unidentified ship of unknown origin. Please signal if any Galactic Confederation ship is in this vicinity. Over."

Meantime, the captain had been jotting down his observations. He was now grumbling in a worried way: "I'm not getting any answer to my calls to the unidentified flying object. It is not emitting any radiation and its engines are not working. We'll have to try getting inside to inspect it."

"Look, don't you think it would be more sensible

to wait for an answer from the President? Maybe the Great Council can give us information. After all, this could easily have come from the planet Neos where we have a base," Pentoser argued.

"You don't honestly believe that the Great Council is going to consult the Great Brains there?" Setni scoffed. But Pentoser said, "Theoretically, no. The great Brains of our deceased scientists are not usually bothered with trifles. Perhaps it is an experiment?"

"In that case, Kalapol will notify us," Setni replied. "Personally, I don't think so. Look at its shape. It certainly is not the product of any spaceship plant on Pollux."

Pentoser said, "Suppose it's been sent out by the Psyborgs? Kampl ought to be warned immediately!"

I'm not going to disturb the President of the whole Confederation until I have more information. I'll put on my space suit and go out to get a closer look at this ship."

"You should wait for orders from Kalapol!" Pentoser was annoyed. "They will be sent soon; you can relay them to me," Setni replied.

"Well, be careful. Remember what happened to you on Planet 2928 of Hydra. No one ever understood the meaning of your adventures in that archaic world. We never heard another word about those Psyborgs. If I hadn't known you so well, I'd have thought you imagined all your adventures in that medieval world. I've never understood how disembodied spirits could be programmed by a computer..."[1]

"You've zeroed in on the problem. You see, I still dream about that planet of the Psyborgs, especially my lovely Nicolette. So, if this ship is something sent by Wotan, Oberon and Dahut, I want to know about it. Oh, if it only were... I'm fed up with these dull patrols. At least here's something new, so, I'm reconnoitering. See you soon," Setni said happily.

"Good luck! Be careful."

Setni smiled as he prepared to leave. His mind was filled with the faces of those he had loved on that marvelous planet: the brave knight Huon de Bordeaux and the gentle, golden-haired Nicolette. A few moments later, the tall astronaut had donned his space suit. From his belt hung a disintegrator to enable him to enter the hull of the floating ship. Just then, their answer from Kalapol came through.

"Captain Setni is hereby ordered to find out the identity of the unknown craft. There are no ships from Pollux in that area. A squadron is now headed in your direction. President Kampl is most anxious that no hostile act should occur. In case of danger, the *Zineb* should head for the Planet Neos. Roger. Over."

"Orders loud and clear," Pentoser responded at once. "Captain Setni is going to try to board the ship. Please listen..."

Captain Setni smiled, thinking the Admiralty

---

[1] *Games Psyborgs Play* by the same author.

had believed the incident important enough to warrant the attention of the President himself! That might earn him a promotion if he accomplished the mission. The Great Council apparently had believed in his adventures with the Psyborgs. They seemed to be just as interested in clearing up the mystery.

He fastened his helmet, then pressed the valve to empty the air lock. When the pressure was at zero, he opened the exit, dropped into space and moved away from the *Zineb*.

"Hello! Testing!" He heard Pentoser's voice, "Can you hear me?"

"Yes," Setni answered.

"Tell me about what you see as you proceed. If there is any trouble, return on the double."

"OK! I'm using the thrusters on my backpack. Everything is A-OK. I'm now getting close to the hull. That's queer; the surface looks perfectly smooth. There's not a ripple, nor a crack in it. It's impossible to figure out how it is propelled. Just a minute, I'm going to move around it . . ." Setni continued, "No, I've never seen anything like this. It's like an egg. It may not even have an air lock."

A few seconds elapsed, then the astronaut spoke again: "Ah! There's an orange circle. That must be the entrance. I'm getting closer. There is a red knob in the center. OK! I'm pushing it open ... Good! It *is* the way into the ship, but the door has mysteriously disappeared. That brings back memories. Pentoser, I shouldn't be surprised if the Psyborgs haven't shown up again! I'm entering the air-lock. Don't worry if communication is cut off. Unless something unforeseen happens, I'll be back in half an hour. 'Bye!"

Pentoser did not answer because communication had ceased when Setni moved to the other side of the unknown craft. Meanwhile, the captain had entered the hull.

The Polluxian then set out on his exploration. The air lock opened onto a vast and brightly lit corridor. Not a living soul, no exits, not a single instrument to be seen. The light came directly from the walls.

Weapon in hand, Setni proceeded cautiously along the corridor. His earphones picked up no sound except the soft padding of his own boots on a floor smooth as glass. Suddenly, an opening appeared on a partition to his left. There was a large cabin, containing only one armchair, placed dead center.

Hesitating a second, the astronaut entered this room. The opening sealed itself hermetically behind him. Feeling the wall with his hand, he detected not a crack. Shrugging his shoulders, now he eyed the armchair suspiciously. As he took a few steps toward it, a bell-like voice startled him.

The melodious laugh reverberated like an echo in a deep valley. Setni's heart began to thump wildly; in the whole Galaxy only Nicolette laughed like that. The voice took him back to the happy days of his courtship, when he pursued his limpid-eyed love through the cool countryside of the Psyborg planet.

But his mind warned him that he must be wrong. Hadn't the Psyborgs told him, long ago, that this fair damsel was an android technologically created by them? Yes, he was recalling everything; she had forgotten him even before she disappeared from the planet on which she had led only an ephemeral existence. Had those all-powerful lords reversed their decision? Had they decided to restore a body and memory to the golden-haired lady?

Surely not! He must be hallucinating, though his helmet was equipped to protect him from such attacks. What was he to believe?

At once, the walls of the cabin appeared translucent, then became an endless succession of mirrors. All reflected the same face: Nicolette.

Wild with joy, arms outstretched, Setni rushed toward that image. His hands reached into empty space. The sweet girl had disappeared, only to reappear in another facet of the prism.

Filled with desire, the astronaut ran around in pursuit of the image, just out of his reach. Nicolette's arms stretched out toward him, beckoning him to enter her enchanted world in the mirror. The poor man doggedly kept bumping into a wall.

At last, the cruel game ended. Exhausted, the Polluxian realized the futility of his efforts and dropped into the armchair.

A fantastic vision materialized instantly: there were three crystal thrones. In the first, sat a fabulously beautiful woman, her long black hair cascading down her golden tunic. In the second, was a dwarf of unearthly beauty, wearing a silver-embroidered jerkin. In the last sat a gloomy-faced giant, with piercing eyes; he wore a leather belt from which hung a long sword.

This time, Setni had no further doubts: he recognized the all-powerful Psyborgs whom he had met long ago. They were Dahut, Queen of the city of Ys; Oberon, the fairyland dwarf who ruled the City of Clouds, and Wotan the Fearless, ruler of subterranean worlds.

Then two other forms materialized, to come smilingly toward him; a knight in armor and an adorable young blonde. "Nicolette," the astronaut cried out, "is it really you, my love?"

"Dearest," the apparition murmured, nestling next to him. "We're together again, after so long..."

They locked in a tight embrace, passionately kissing madly while the four others watched. When they finally separated, Setni threw his arm around the knight. "Huon, my friend! How happy I am to see you."

Deeply touched, the knight hugged him. "I've missed you, brave Setni. I knew you wouldn't forget us! Unfortunately, we couldn't get a message to you."

"This time, I hope we won't part so soon," answered the Polluxian, addressing the three rulers still seated on their thrones.

"We were touched by your love, Setni," Dahut said, smiling. "That's why we decided to give you another chance to see the woman you love so much."

"I am ready, if necessary, to give up my own country to serve you until I die!"

"We're not asking that much!" Oberon laughed. "However, if you want Nicolette back, you'll have to undertake a difficult mission for us."

"Anything, as long as she is mine," the astronaut answered, impulsively.

"We value your courage, Setni!" Wotan interrupted. "That's why we decided to summon you; only a human can travel where we want you to go."

"Tell me! If it is possible to carry out your mission, it shall be done."

"Don't commit yourself without hearing me out, dear friend," Oberon went on. "You're free to refuse. The situation is this: our people were wiped out long ago by an epidemic; for many years we thought that the sudden appearance and mutation of the virus responsible for their deaths had been produced by evil creatures who hated humankind. For aeons, we wandered along the Milky Way, on the lookout for any indication of a new attack by them on others. We never discovered anything. However, a short time ago, we spotted a new planet that bears a strange resemblance to the one you once saw. Was it a sort of planetary stage, with no past or future, controlled solely by the minds of other Psyborgs like us?

"In spite of our powers, we have been unable to find out the real origin of its inhabitants. Evil creatures rule this star who can manipulate matter and time. What are they doing in this galaxy? Perhaps they are waiting for your compatriots to contact them? Unfortunately, the weapons of Polluxians are useless against their psychic science. That's why we thought of sending you there, to size up the situation. Your previous experience has made you familiar with phantasmagoric control of the mind; you are the only one who can shed further light on this mystery."

"I see," the astronaut replied, "but couldn't you have sent an android like Huon de Bordeaux, who is afraid of nothing?"

"Naturally, we thought of it," Oberon said, approvingly. "But we were afraid they might suspect our existence. I repeat, only a creature of flesh and bone, born in the Galaxy, can reach that planet. He will become the target of powerful, evil forces. If he succeeds, those accursed people will fear him and all his descendants. Don't worry, you will have our full support to aid you. First, take this belt for your sword; it has a cabochon that will enable you to change your shape at will. It can magnify tenfold your psychic powers. We will seal your mind against the power of your enemies, but beware: no atomic weapon, no disintegrator will work there. You will discover a medieval civilization which serves as a cover for evil. Those are false props used to conceal demons who want to experiment with the human psyche. You will feel bewildered, you often won't grasp the significance of events; your best guides will be your courage and integrity. Are you still willing to take the assignment?"

"I must say, your story intrigues me. Even without the prospect of seeing Nicolette, I'd take it because I'm inquisitive."

"We expected that, Setni!" Wotan exclaimed. "To show our good faith, you may live for a year with Nicolette on the planet Hydra, which you already know. Then, you will begin your mission."

Don't you think I'd better start out at once?"

"Oh Setni!" said Dahut, laughing. "Don't worry. That year will actually last an instant; your mission will not be delayed by it."

"It would be foolish to refuse," the astronaut replied. "But I'd like a guarantee that our reunion will be real."

"Don't ask for too much, my friend," Oberon replied. "You know she loves you, but you both belong to different worlds. You'll see her again later, we swear; but you'll have to leave her again in the future."

The Polluxian grasped Nicolette's slender hand, sighing. "Oh, my sweet, our love can't last, yet just the prospect of having you to myself for a whole year is enough. I agree . . ."

Thereupon, the bare cabin of the spaceship disappeared. Setni found himself once more living on the Eden-like planet of Hydra where he had first met Nicolette. He spent a happy year with her and his friend Huon de Bordeaux. Finally, on the evening of the last day, he said good-bye and boarded a spaceship exactly like the *Zineb*.

The crossing was very short, and two days after his departure, he saw a golden star grow perceptibly larger. Soon, the ship landed gently on a green field; then it took off, leaving its passenger.

Setni found himself mounted on a coal-black charger, his lance in hand, sword hanging from his side. He spurred his charger to a gallop and dashed on to the plain. His new mission had just started: was he going to live up to the Psyborgs' expectations?

Chapter I

As he rode along, Setni took in deep breaths of fresh air, while watching alertly for danger. Surrounding him were green pastures, dotted with small groves of trees. The atmosphere was oppressively hot, a few black clouds were rapidly approaching: a storm was brewing.

Goshawks were circling in the muggy air, searching for prey: occasionally one would plummet to earth, then fly up, holding in its talons some poor rabbit. Often a hare, alarmed by the sound of hooves, streaked out. There was no sign of human habitation.

The astronaut began to examine the equipment he received from the Psyborgs: his resplendent breast-plate and shield were embossed with an azure cross moline. His meshed gauntlets were remarkably supple, as were his sollerets. All this armor must have been specially made. He pulled his sword partly out of its scabbard, admiring its sharp edge, wondering if his skill in handling it was as great as it used to be. He was suddenly flooded with memories; he recalled the numerous passages at

THE ENCHANTED PLANET

arms with his friend, Huon. He could still feel the lunges and parries, saw the jousts with long lances heard the clatter of metal, the sudden movement of his horse as he turned to charge. He knew where all the joints in the armor were. He thought gratefully of the Psyborgs. He reined in: far to the left he saw a strange procession of three persons approaching.

Was this to be his first test? His heart thumping, the astronaut scanned their faces. The first was a solidly-build knight of noble bearing, sitting erect in his saddle. His armor shone, his silver buckler bore marks of many battles. A purple cross, much like Setni's, adorned his breastplate. His charger was gnawing at a foam-covered bit.

Slightly behind him came an aristocratic lady, seated on a snow white horse. A tulle veil, cascading from her hennin, partly covered her attractive, sad face. The folds of her long black dress were draped over the horse's flank. Trailing behind them, a curious dwarf whom Setni took for some mutant, rode a snow-white donkey. His mount staggered under the weight of baggage. The dwarf appeared as sad as the lady.

Setni, bracing for action, tightened his knees, loosened his sword and raised his shield protectively. But the knight's intentions seemed friendly. He stopped his horse at some distance from Setni and, raising his right arm, hailed his peer:

"Greetings to you, Sir Knight! May I ask your name?" "Certainly," the envoy from the Psyborgs replied courteously. "I am the Knight of the Azure Cross. And you?"

"I am the Knight of the Purple Cross," he answered. "We could easily be brothers-at-arms, since our emblems differ only in color. May I present Unia, the lady of my heart?"

"You must believe, noble lady, I have never met anyone lovelier!" the Knight of the Azure Cross stated. "Surely such beauty must inspire tenfold the valor of your knight."

Unia smiled, bowing her head slightly, a faint rosy color tinted her pale cheeks. Though susceptible to this gallant hommage, she retained a royal dignity. "You certainly know, sir, how to flatter a lady," grumbled the Knight of the Purple Cross. "But it's true that I shall need my strength during my present endeavor. I have sworn to Lady Unia that I will free her parents, the prisoners of vile sorcerers." "A noble quest! A valiant knight should certainly be able..." Setni interrupted.

"Alas! If it were only fighting you would be right, my friend. But, a fire-breathing dragon guards them, night and day. Courage is not enough to face such a foe," Purple Cross cried. "I understand your plight. Will you permit me to accompany you? I have also sworn to combat monsters and sorcerers. You are giving me a chance to fulfill that vow," Setni answered.

Purple Cross said, "I accept with pleasure! Thank you for your offer. Two swords are better than one. I'll wager ours will never grow rusty," Setni, now Knight of the Azure Cross, replied. "Well, let us not keep that fiendish beast waiting!"

So the small procession continued the journey.

The two knights conversed, keeping a worried eye on the heavy clouds above. Finally, they came to a shady wood. The dense foliage kept out the summer heat; the shade was refreshing. Setni, intrigued, asked his companion to identify the various trees.

"Sir Knight, you must come from a faraway country not to know them! Do you see that slender tree trunk, pointing to the sky? That is the pine which provides sailors with masts to sail their ships. This one is the oak, king of the forest, whose strength has defied violent hurricanes. Over there, that dark green is the somber cypress; this is the fragrant laurel whose leaves are woven into crowns to adorn the brows of conquerors. The mournful willow which droops its branches toward the ground is the emblem of jilted lovers. Admire the holly-oak, favorite of sculptors, for it's fine for the most delicate carving. Finally, there's the birch from which are fashioned battle arrows projected by bows of flexible yew."

"I thank you for the valuable information. Note how the birds have stopped singing. I hear thunder. Large rain drops are falling on the trees. Would it not be wise to find shelter for Lady Unia?"

"Assuredly, though the thick foliage will afford us some shelter, but the violence of a storm will soon pierce it. Unfortunately, like you, I'm a stranger here. I don't know whether there is some castle nearby. Let us hurry."

They spurred their horses to a trot: behind them the dwarf grimaced, fearful of getting lost in the forest. Thunderclaps soon echoed in the forest; continual flashes of lightning blinded the travelers. The rain lashed their armor and streamed down the flanks of their mounts. Whirlwinds of leaves circled in the wind, like butterflies.

Soon they came to a vast clearing at the end of which was a dark cavern. The knights paused, to give the dwarf time to catch up. Purple Cross dismounted and, handing his lance to the dwarf, started entering the grotto to make sure no savage beast was inside.

Then the Lady Unia cried out: "Beware, dear friend! This looks familiar to me. It is the lair of a horrendous monster who unhinges the minds of unfortunates who seek shelter there."

"Let's flee!" the dwarf said. "In this accursed grotto, no living being can conquer the monster. It is invincible Error . . ." But Purple Cross did not heed him. Bold and eager, he unsheathed his sword and stepped toward the dark entrance. Setni dismounted and, placing his faith in the Psyborgs, was ready to help.

The words of the lady and of the dwarf had been true: the monster could control the brain of humans. The outcome of battle did not really depend on the valor of the knights. They had to resist the false images which Error would conjure up in their minds. Was Purple Cross aware of the risk he was running? Could he repulse the suggestions of his foe?

The Knight of the Purple Cross, brandishing his sword, boldly stepped into the cavern, followed by Setni. It took a moment for their eyes to adjust to

THE ENCHANTED PLANET

the semi-darkness. There they saw a repulsive creature with female breasts and a serpent's body, terminating in a venomous pointed tail. Around her teemed innumerable small replicas of Error, her children. As soon as those repellent animals saw the two knights, they took refuge in the gaping jaws of their mother, where they vanished.

Outside, the thunder rumbled with increasing loudness. The lightning flashes were reflected on the knights' shiny breastplates, dazzling the she-demon who retreated, coiling up in rings, to the back of her lair. Error darted her scaly tail and threatened Purple Cross with her hideous jaws, but he did not retreat. Brandishing his sword, he rushed his adversary and struck a powerful blow. The blade slid along the viscous head, cutting deep into her shoulder.

Howling like the damned, Error then stretched out her powerful body. She coiled herself about Purple Cross, pinning him within her sinking folds; he could not move.

Azure Cross rushed to his rescue. Raising his sword in both hands he was prepared to strike; but suddenly instead of the disgusting beast he saw a most beautiful woman, Nicolette. . . . A glowing smile upon her lips, her arms were stretched out toward him invitingly. Setni, like an automaton, took one step forward, then others. He was within reach of the poisonous tail when another flash of lightning lit up the grotto. Unia, who was watching, uttered a shriek of despair. The vision vanished at once.

Setni raised his sword and plunged it into the paunch of the monster. A revolting stream of filth spurted out, filling the cavern with a nauseating stench. Half-digested toads and frogs wriggled about, with the offspring of the monster, squirming in dark slime and attacking the knights! The monsters crawled on the ground, slippery from the revolting dirt gushing forth from the gaping wound. Weakened by the gash in her abdomen, Error slackened her hold. Purple Cross was able to wriggle out of her coils.

The worthy knight, ashamed of his defeat before Unia, dealt the monster another furious blow. He severed the monstrous head which rolled on the rocks, black blood spurting out.

But Error had not yet expired. In a final desperate effort, she tried to befuddle her foes by appearing as a mother, bleeding from multiple wounds surrounded by her crying, cherubic infants. But the monster's life was oozing away and the vision evaporated. In place of the cherubs, there remained the small monsters. They ruthlessly clawed the throat of their dying mother, sucking the blood flowing from her.

Revolted by this hideous spectacle, the two friends redoubled their attack and degutted the little monsters, killing every last one. The two companions then left the beast's lair to join Unia, behind whom cowered the dwarf, pale with fright. The storm had stopped and the birds started to sing again, in the foliage of a tall tree. The sun's rays made the wet leaves sparkle like diamonds.

THE ENCHANTED PLANET

"Brave knights," the Lady Unia exclaimed, "you are so valorous! Your deed has freed the countryside from a powerful monster. There can be no reward great enough for you."

"Sweet friend," Purple Cross replied, "the credit is due to our Azure Cross. Without him, I should have been suffocated by Error. My mind, filled by hallucinations, could see only your beautiful image, instead of the snake coiled about me. He must know that I am forever in his debt!"

"Sir," Azure Cross replied, "it was just a lucky stroke that freed you from that stinking hug. You alone killed the monster Error!"

The knight argued, "But without you, my body would have been crushed by the monster's tail. I never could have killed him." Azure Cross said, "Enough, I am willing to accept your help and shall call upon you if need be. Now, let us continue on our way."

They both remounted and the little group followed a grassy path which seemed to lead out of the wood. Despite his seeming confidence, Setni was worried. Both he and Purple Cross had inhaled, during combat, the terrible odors vomited by Error. They were probably powerful hallucinogens; inoculated by the Psyborgs, he had nothing to fear. But his unfortunate friend might momentarily lose his sanity. He would have to observe him.

Meanwhile, he decided to learn what he could about this strange country. "You know that I am a stranger to this part of the country," he said,

"Would you tell me more about yourself and others like you. Where were you born?"

"Gentle companion, your question baffles me! I don't know how to answer it . . ." Purple Cross murmured. "Who were your parents? Where did they live?" Setni questioned.

"That is of little interest. I was taken from my mother at birth, like everyone else in this country. We have no recollections of our childhood . . . We learn to bear arms and our lives are one long series of trials and suffering. It comes to an end only when our lords decide . . ."

"You amaze me, friend," Setni replied. "Those lords strike me as being so cruel. What happens when you displease these sovereigns?"

"We are punished: monsters like Error settle among us. Humans undergo long torment, until one of us succeeds in killing them. Unfortunately, that's almost impossible, which is why your recent victory fills us with admiration. Perhaps you were sent here to deliver us from our merciless tormentors."

"Have you ever met one of those perverse lords?" Setni asked. "No never! It is said they disguise themselves and live among humans, to test them. But they never reveal themselves," Purple Cross revealed.

"But surely this world has some past history," Setni insisted. But Purple Cross was puzzled. "What do you mean? Always knights have set forth on quests, attempting to wipe out the dragons to relieve our sufferings. Very few succeed, as I've told you."

"Who manufactures your weapons? Who looks after your needs?" Setni continued, curiously. "We find everything we need in our castles. Their attics are always full. If you need a new sword, you just help yourself. The next day, another one appears, to take its place. The rulers attend to that," Purple Cross assured him.

"Have you never wondered who built these castles, harvested the grain, wove your clothes?" Setni demanded. "But everyone knows that: our rulers do. But tell me, are things different in your country?" Purple Cross asked.

Setni laughed, "Unfortunately, yes! Where I live, each man is born ignorant and must learn what his forefathers have learned before him. Only great effort makes it possible to produce the essentials of life." Purple Cross was amazed. "I don't understand! When you want a goblet, some one else must make it for you?"

"Thats' right . . ."

"I feel sorry for you! Your forefathers must have sinned grievously to live in such a pitiable state. It's different here, see . . ." Purple Cross put out his hand and a goblet, filled with bubbly wine, materialized.

"Taste this, my friend; your thirst will be quenched."

Setni drank and the wine did have a marvelous bouquet. "I see that you have no need to harvest grapes! This drink is heavenly. But tell me, if your wishes are instantly fulfilled, why is the donkey staggering under a load of baggage?"

"Oh! It would be unseemly to ask for things we already have. Our coats and doublets are not worn out; we keep them until they must be replaced," Purple Cross explained.

"I must say you live in a strange world. You constantly undergo trials, yet you are free from material concerns. I wish I could understand why!"

"Perhaps our masters will reveal it," the Knight answered, enigmatically. "There surely must be some reason for your presence in our midst."

Setni did not reply: he reasoned that these unfortunate people had been subjected during infancy to some hypnotic treatment that kept them under control by those masters he was constantly hearing about. To what purpose?

The small procession had now left the forest. Just then, a white-bearded, barefoot old man dressed in rough homespun came walking along, beating his breast and praying. He bowed to the knights who responded courteously.

Purple Cross asked: "Tell me, holy man, have you heard of anyone here who needs the services of two knights? We wish to engage in combat, to prove our valor."

"May Heaven preserve me," answered the old man. "It would be unseemly for a hermit, dedicated to prayer, to trouble himself about this base world. However, if you wish to aid a just cause, I have heard pilgrims complain of a blood-thirsty creature who ravages the countryside."

"Speak! Where is he to be found? It would be a great shame not to put an end to his evil deeds.

This is precisely our quest," Purple Cross exclaimed.

"Very well. You must ride for one day toward the rising sun. There, in a small wilderness, you will find the beast."

"My Lords," the Lady Unia said. "These last adventures have been exhausting for me. Night is falling, we have had no rest; your strength will fail. I long to spend a peaceful night in a warm house."

"Your Lordships, that is sensible," the hermit replied. "Your noble companion combines wisdom and beauty. I invite you to rest in my humble abode; you can journey at dawn with renewed vigor."

"I agree," said Purple Cross. "After you, holy man, show us the way."

They reached the bottom of a misty valley near a forest, where the holy man's hermitage was located. The sky shone with the purple and gold of twilight, the last rays of the sun lit the belfry of the small chapel where the hermit prayed. Not far away was a clear stream, its banks surrounded by ghostly fog.

After a frugal meal of nuts and cheese, the knights and the lady spoke with the holy man. His conversation was punctuated by edifying quotations. They soon succumbed to weariness and retired, to fall asleep at once.

As soon as the hermit saw them sunk in deep sleep, he noiselessly crept to a secret cabinet from which he drew a book of spells. He chanted evil incantations which called on Demogordon, the Prince of Darkness, to mislead the minds of his guests with visions. Legions of evil spirits materialized about the sorcerer, whose name was Archimago. They entered the minds of his helpless victims.

Setni was protected by his helmet. Purple Cross, more receptive after the evil fumes he inhaled while battling the monster Error, was the first one to be affected. Setni realized that these visions were the result of hypnosis, but its malevolent power was such that it took all his strength to resist; he could not shield the knight and Unia from it.

A dark cloud hovered over the heads of the sleepers, from which emanated visions. The Knight of the Purple Cross had disturbing dreams: his Unia, whom he had always believed chaste, came toward him nude while Graces danced about her, weaving a garland of flowers.

Unia's imaginary evil double looked at him suggestively, then kissed him with passion. Her white hands wandered up and down his body, while the aroused knight did not know whether to respond to her advances. She murmured tender words in his ear, confessing her desire and entreating his caresses.

The knight's ideal of Unia was so different that he began to resist this voluptuous whore, holding back her expert hands. So the rebuffed, imaginary Unia left, looking deeply disappointed. Purple Cross, thoroughly upset, hesitated to call her back. But the thwarted succubus would not admit defeat.

She approached the knight again. He was startled to see a ghostly double of himself, issuing from his own body. He took her in his arms, covering her with kisses. He stretched her out on his monastic pallet and enjoyed the greatest pleasures of the flesh.

When the she-demon left him exhausted, she gave herself to the Knight of the Azure Cross, Setni. So, until dawn, the evil rulers of the planet played with the minds of the two knights.

Setni was conscious, but unable to break the spell. He despaired at his own weakness. It seemed that he was going to fail in his mission.

In the morning, when rosy-fingered dawn had dispelled the darkness, Purple Cross woke. He was still under the demon's spell and thought he saw Unia resting in Setni's arms. Enraged, he unsheathed his sword to wound his faithless companion. But Setni, with tremendous effort, recovered his full psychic powers. He paralyzed the avenging arm, then hastily dressing, rushed out of the hut. His horse was waiting for him peacefully grazing in the dewy grass; Setni leapt upon his back and fled from the cursed dwelling to avoid fighting his entranced friend.

As soon as Purple Cross had been released from paralysis, he followed Setni, accompanied by the dwarf. He left behind the woman whom he now looked upon as a wanton. Unia woke up in the deserted hut. She saw no trace of the hermit, nor of the two knights. Thoroughly puzzled, she left the enchanted valley and tried to follow the tracks of the horses.

Setni had no trouble in tricking his pursuers, for

their minds were still fuzzy. He returned to the valley, intending to rescue Unia from the magician.

To his great surprise he saw an image of Purple Cross riding with Unia. Touching his cabochon, Setni concentrated his psychic powers and succeeded in dispelling the deception. It dissipated in gusts of smoke. Unia, baffled, had watched.

"My Lord," cried the unfortunate woman, "help me! Am I possessed by a wicked sorcerer? Why did my companion disappear? I always behaved prudently. Please tell me."

"My lady," the knight assured her, "your conduct has been above reproach. Unfortunately, our friend's mind was unhinged by the poisonous exhalations of the monster Error. That hermit was really a demonic sorcerer, Archimago. Last night, terrible dreams misled Purple Cross who, convinced we had both betrayed his friendship, rushed out in pursuit of me. Luckily, I was able to escape and rescue you from the power of Archimago. He had summoned up an image of Purple Cross, to ride by your side. You need not fear his evil power; I am at your service and we shall try to discover what happened to your unfortunate knight."

"I accept gratefully, Sir Knight, but how are we going to follow him?"

"Fortunately, dear lady, I also have certain powers. See, in this gem I wear, the trail of the knight we seek. Let us hurry, for he may again succumb to that vile Archimago."

Setni's thoughts wandered. "If Pentoser could see me now, with this beautiful girl, he wouldn't believe it. This enchanted planet is certainly playing tricks on me! I've been talking in jargon which would make astronauts laugh, yet I feel perfectly at ease among these anachronistic phantasms. I hope all this will be explained later. Meantime, I must play the game."

They galloped through the countryside fresh with morning scents. Over hill and dale they rode, until noon. Setni kept hurrying his companion, for disquieting images were constantly appearing on his cabochon. The perfidious Archimago did not consider himself beaten and was plotting new troubles. He would have to use all the powers of the Psyborgs to stop that damned magician.

Chapter II

Indeed, Purple Cross and the dwarf had encountered a couple conjured up by the sorcerer: the Knight of Little Faith and a fair lady, Duessa. She was actually a witch, an accomplice of Archimago, who wanted to cast a spell over Purple Cross to make him forget Unia.

Purple Cross, raging at the unfaithfulness of friends, instantly challenged Little Faith. He accepted the duel at once. They hurried off in opposite directions, turned and charged at one another, lances pointed. The weapons, firmly held, simultaneously struck each shield. The two adversaries were unhorsed and fell with a clatter of metal. Purple Cross, whose mind was still befuddled, rose with difficulty. Fortunately for him, Little Faith had sprained an ankle and was limping badly.

As the horses trotted off to graze, the knights battled once more, dealing each other vigorous slashes and thrusts. The clash of weapons on armor resounded. The dwarf cowered, holding his head in his hands. Duessa, on the other hand, seemed to enjoy the joust, whose prize she was. She encouraged each combatant in turn.

Purple Cross had one distinct advantage: he could move with ease, where Little Faith had to pivot narrowly to parry the blows that were raining upon him from all directions. His left wrist received such a hit that he dropped his shield and was unable to pick it up, while his adversary closed in upon him. Now he tried only to defend himself.

The outcome of the struggle was no longer in doubt. Little Faith begged for mercy. For a moment, Purple Cross hesitated, his fury urging him to kill anyone who challenged him. However, his chivalrous spirit came to the fore, so he let the vanquished knight go. The latter abandoned his shield and limped to his charger.

Purple Cross signaled to the dwarf to pick up the discarded shield and went to pay his homage to the beautiful, evil Duessa. Smiling, she offered him her scarf. The knight accepted this gratefully and tied it to the point of his lance. They trotted off together while the defeated knight disappeared into the mist.

Despite his former love for Unia, Purple Cross thought he had never met so marvelously beautiful a lady. Her full lips invited kisses, her lily and rose complexion was peerless; her firm, half-covered breasts, straining at her bodice were tempting. An intoxicating sandalwood perfume made her beauty seem even more irresistible. The knight, having decided to reveal his love, dismounted near a weeping willow. He wanted to weave a crown for this queen of beauty.

To his intense surprise, a piercing scream resounded in the woods. He exclaimed, "What wondrous thing is this? This tree complains like a human, suffering from a dreadful wound."

"Pay no attention to that, dear friend," answered Duessa with a bewitching smile. "It's a trick played by a magician who wants to test you. Come, my heart's delight, I can hardly wait to feel your arms about me. A marvelous palace awaits us, where we can enjoy our happiness."

She spurred her palfrey on, leading the way. Purple Cross, wonder-struck, observed the scarlet bead trickling from the broken tree limb. Shaking his head, he remounted and hurried to follow Duessa. The dwarf, terror-stricken, fled in the opposite direction. He soon met Setni and Unia who were tracking the enchanted knight. The three rode on toward the wounded tree. Setni could not help feeling deeply attracted toward the woman whom he had possessed in his dreams. Deciding to demonstrate the power of his own magic gifts, he observed:

"See, gentle lady, in what terrible way this sorceress betrayed an unfortunate lover! This willow conceals a lover who, having fallen in love with Duessa, realized her evil and spat out his scorn. She took her revenge in this manner, imprisoning him."

"Is that true, gentle knight? Free him if it is in your power," Unia pleaded.

Setni looked away from the cabochon that had allowed him to detect the human form in the tree. Focusing his mind, he entreated the Psyborgs to give back to this mutant his original shape. Then, the leaves fell slowly to the ground, as though blown by an autumnal wind. The slender stems clustered together as the bark of the trunk lost its roughness. The features of a sad face appeared in ghostly fashion, in the middle of the tree. A few moments later, a handsome adolescent was standing where the willow had been. He made a clumsy gesture, took a few faltering steps and threw himself at the feet of his rescuer.

"May the Lord bless you, sir! Without you, I should have spent the remainder of my days in that misery. The accursed Duessa, who transformed me, just now went by me accompanied by a knight. May Heaven have mercy on him. That cruel woman will undo him with a powerful spell and he will be accursed forever."

Setni retorted with determination, "I shall not rest until I have put an end to her evil deeds!"

"Gentle sir, may you attain your goal. But don't abandon me; if that cruel woman finds me she will cast another spell on me," the boy begged.

"Very well, you may come with us. Better still, lead us to some dwelling where we may find food."

"With pleasure, gentle sir! I know a good woman who lives not far from here; she will extend her hospitality to us."

The friends continued on their way through the verdant countryside. The boy soon pointed to a ribbon of smoke rising above the trees. Then they saw a tidy little cottage, where two women who seemed to be awaiting their guests were by the door.

On the way, Setni had been mulling over the situation: two magicians, Archimago and Duessa, seemed to dominate all the inhabitants they met. If he wanted to confront the sorceress, he could not burden himself with Unia. Furthermore, the sweet girl seemed to have fallen in love with him; she looked at him, blushing whenever he spoke to her. Setni wasn't sure he could remain faithful to Nicolette.

Taking stock of the psychic powers which the Psyborgs had bestowed upon him, powers of which he had not really been sure, he had come to a decision to fight the magicians.

"Fair Unia," he said, "I cannot allow you to run such risks. It ill befits a noble lady to wander the countryside in the company of a knight. I think you had better wait for me here. This boy and two pleasant women can keep you company.

"Is this your farewell, Azure Cross?" murmured the lady. "How can you contemplate leaving me defenseless, to withstand the sorcerers who haunt this region? Have I failed you in some way? Tell me, I beseech you . . ."

"Fair lady. I never entertained the idea of leaving you unprotected. Look . . ." Setni rubbed his cabochon—the most marvelous gadget he had ever used—and a lion with a heavy mane materialized.

At this sight, Unia was terrified. "Fear not, my lady. This beast will never harm you. He will serve you faithfully and will not allow anyone to harm you. He can forestall any evil and deal with any trouble."

"Will he be able to ward off spells cast by Archimago and Duessa?" Unia asked.

"I hope so. In any event, I shan't be long; that is my fondest hope."

The pseudo knight then took his leave. The dwarf followed Setni.

Unfortunately, the lion summoned up by Setni was not equal to his task: the astronaut had familiarized himself with the psychic powers of the Psyborgs, but he still had much to learn. Shortly after his departure, a robber came to the cottage and the lion instantly went after him. The magician, taking advantage of Setni's absence, conjured up an image of the man Unia still loved, the Knight of the Purple Cross.

As soon as she saw him, the poor girl, overjoyed, rushed forward with outstretched arms. The magic lion disappeared. Once more, Unia was in the clutches of Archimago.

"Gentle knight," murmured the lady, "I was pining for you. You were upset by evil visions and left me, but I've never forgotten you. Your presence here makes me rejoice!"

"Madam, let us forget my misunderstanding," the pseudo-Purple Cross replied glibly. "Monstrous Error deranged my mind, but the fresh scent of the woods cleans the noxious miasmas that poisoned me. Yes, I love you and I shall never more leave you. Come, let us go from this humble cottage to a dwelling more worthy of our felicity."

Rosy with pleasure, Unia collected her belongings and after a hasty farewell to her hostesses, mounted her palfrey to follow her love. The knight and the lady galloped down the path which Setni had followed a short while before. As they rode along, never had Unia, who was transfigured with joy, found her suitor so tender and attentive. A steady stream of praises poured from the knight's lips; he repeatedly squeezed her delicate hand in his own strong one and kissed it, looking intently into Unia's eyes.

Fortunately, Setni was watching them. His cabochon showed him a scene which astonished him. Surely, Purple Cross was not with Unia, for the image had shown him to be with a ravishing lady who had seduced him.

Therefore, Unia's companion could only have been conjured up by the malevolent magicians. Pulling his charger around so suddenly that the noble steed reared with a cry of pain, Setni retraced his steps at top speed.

The noon sun beat down on his armor and Setni was sweating freely under his metal collar. But he paid no attenion, being alarmed about saving poor Unia.

Disregarding groups of graceful fawns and driads who were disporting themselves in the soft shade, he spurred on his steed through briar and copse, scattering clouds of dust. This combat would surely be to the finish. Only one thing mattered: freeing Unia.

It did not take him long to find the couple. When the pseudo-Purple Cross caught sight of the knight rushing at him, lance at the ready, he simply disappeared. The beautiful Unia found herself alone, amazed.

"What, Sir Knight!" she exclaimed. "Your coming made my valiant companion go up in smoke. What strange magic!"

"Gentle lady, be not surprised. Purple Cross is really far away, with the witch Duessa. It was Archimago the magician who accompanied you; he was trying to take advantage of you."

"Sir Knight, I am in your debt. Had you not come, more spells would have been cast over me! You are a thousand times more competent than my poor Purple Cross, who allows himself to be tricked so easily. What would happen to me without you? Speak, dear friend, I am yours."

These words excited Setni, who had already found Unia very appealing. His mind in a whirl, he led her under the foliage where they lay side by side, caressing each other. But Unia's impassioned moans attracted a strange herd roaming the woods. These mutants, half-goat and half-man, did not usually meddle in human affairs, but they liked to play tricks on anyone who entered their domain. Pushing aside Setni, they took Unia away with them.

He set off in pursuit, but soon lost all trace of the mutants. He had to retrace his steps, lest he lose his way in the thick underbrush. As he rode along, he took gloomy stock of the situation: he had been a discredit to those who sent him. Unaccustomed to using psychic powers instead of nuclear weapons, he had made many mistakes.

After all, beautiful as she was, what was Unia to him? Nicolette was his true love. Once more, Archimago had manipulated him. Seducing Unia was another distraction to which he had almost succumbed. Archimago and Duessa were manipulating Purple Cross and Unia, as though they were puppets. Therefore, he had better stop worrying about their fate and concentrate on the rulers of this strange planet. Setni mentally thanked the Psyborgs for having conjured up that band of laughing fawns. Firmly resolved not to be tricked, he decided to find the demonic Duessa's hiding place.

Setni checked his cabochon and a picture of the witch appeared on its diminutive screen: she was riding alongside Purple Cross. They were approaching a marvelous, turreted castle. As they approached the barbican, heralds in crimson doublets welcomed them with their trumpets. Purple Cross, dazzled by this display, unhesitatingly entered the fortification. The drawbridge pulled up behind him.

Setni was then unable to see what was going on behind the walls. He decided to risk going there, despite the powerful spells that probably protected the castle. Before leaving, he sent away the dwarf: "Go, little one! Seek out Lady Unia. Tell her that I am going to try to save the man she loves." The gnome left without further ado.

Setni again used his cabochon, which once more proved invaluable by showing him the location of Duessa's castle. He went off at a gallop, determined this time not to be fooled. He reached the massive fortification just as the sky was glowing with the colors of sunset.

He could see guards silhouetted against the battlements. Strangely, they ignored the dust-covered stranger before the drawbridge. Setni, shouting to no avail, saw an oliphant encrusted with gems that hung by a gold chain on the gate. Seething with rage, he grabbed it and blew as hard as he could.

Duessa finally showed herself. Setni saw her hennin outlined against the rampart as she shouted: "Go on your way, Knight! How dare you disturb me. Know that anyone who enters Lucifera never comes out. Go back to where you came from. Don't challenge powers greater than yours!"

"I care naught for your boasting," Setni replied haughtily. "You are detaining a friend of mine whom I have sworn to wrest from your claws. Open the door, accursed one!"

"So, Sir Knight, since you want to show your powers, make it disappear!" sneered Duessa, going back inside.

Thus challenged, the envoy of the Psyborgs once more used his cabochon. Concentrating on the obstacle, he decided to make it disintegrate. To his surprise, the thick wall slowly became translucent, then transparent and disappeared without a trace.

His joy was short-lived: a horseman mounted on a sturdy charger began to cross the drawbridge. As it was lowered over the moat, his foe pointed his lance at him shouting: "On guard, filthy vermin! There will be no quarter given in this joust!"

Setni hesitated a second; he recognized the voice

and the purple emblem on the shield. "I won't fight you, friend," he assured him. "You have been bewitched by the witch Duessa. I have come to set you free. Let me enter!"

"By all the devils in hell, it will be over my dead body! En garde . . ." Purple Cross aimed his lance and rushed at his former companion.

Setni was on guard and unflinchingly waited for the blow. But he had no intention of wounding his friend, so when the latter neared him, Setni flattened himself on his horse's neck. The blade slid along his back without harming him. "Be reasonable!" he cried. "I don't mean you harm. You've been seduced by a witch. All I want is to free you from her."

"On guard, traitor! You betrayed my friendship with Unia. Only your blood can wash away your offense," the madman replied as he turned. This time, unfortunately, Setni was unable to parry the blow. The lance struck the very center of his shield. The impact was such that he felt himself lifted from his saddle. Whirling helplessly through the air, he landed on his back.

Seeing this, his adversary lunged at him again, ready to pierce his body. Setni rolled over and managed to avoid the thrust, but his back hurt so that he realized he could not last much longer. Purple Cross, having decided to finish the combat, dismounted and discarded his lance. Raising his two-handed sword, he prepared to split the vanquished man's head.

The envoy of the Psyborgs was in difficulty and

could not get up. All he could do was to parry the blows with his sword. Twice he managed, but the third time, he was struck in the shoulder.

"This time I'm done for," Setni thought desperately. "Ah, if only I could become invisible!" To his surprise, he suddenly disappeared.

Purple Cross, frustrated, hit blindly to right and left, while his adversary ran away on all fours. While the knight continued to look for him, mouthing foul epithets, Setni was able to get back on his feet and cross the bridge.

He had unfortunately forgotten about Duessa. He became visible again and once within the walls, he was magically lifted from the ground and carried away. He felt himself fall headlong down a spiral staircase and finally was hurled into a dark, damp cell.

Once more his psychic powers had been foiled by the witch. But perhaps hope was not lost. Had the dwarf found Unia and told her where he was? But what could the poor girl do against the powerful Duessa?

Setni could only wait. He surveyed his prison: it contained a filthy pallet, a jug and some mouldy bread. Rats ran about him and moans, issuing from other cells, attested to his not being the witch's only prisoner.

His situation was certainly deteriorating. His demonic foes were immune to standard weapons and his psychic powers were not sufficiently well developed. Sunk in despair, Setni lay down and drifted into a troubled sleep filled with hideous nightmares.

He was burned by the flames of an inferno, suffering a thousand deaths. Pincers and firebrands tore mercilessly at his flesh. His tormentors, deaf to his entreaties, jeered as they flogged him. The worst part was that he knew he was hallucinating. Sometimes he succeeded in repelling the visions, but each time Duessa's power thrust him back into his endless nightmare.

He thought his fellow sufferers were undergoing the same torments. He thought he saw Purple Cross watching this spectacle. Panic-stricken, he fled the accursed castle, pursued by Duessa in the shape of a huge bat. The witch caught up with him, cast her spell and hurled him down into a dungeon cell.

Then Setni saw a giant mutant cross the drawbridge. He was riding a horrible dragon vomiting flames. Duessa's accomplice, Archimago, had joined up with her.

How was he to repel the assaults on his mind? Once more, infernal legions rushed at him, inflicting unbearable tortures. As despair mounted, Setni placed his hand over his cabochon. The sickening apparitions disappeared in smoke, leaving a nauseous odor of brimstone. A greenish sphere now enveloped Setni; he now saw the stones of his cell.

Then a thin ray of crimson light coiled around the cell gratings, which vanished in a cluster of sparks. There was now nothing to keep Setni prisoner. Thanks to the Psyborgs' miraculous gadget, he had cleansed his mind of the evil

THE ENCHANTED PLANET

images implanted by the two magicians. Still enveloped in his luminescent aura, he climbed the spiral staircase and came out into the castle courtyard. He had no idea for how long he had been in his cell. For a moment, he was blinded by the bright rays of the sun. Then as his eyes became accustomed to the dazzling light, he saw before him the giant mutant and the dragon, awaiting him, ready for battle.

Setni finally understood: he would never win by force of arms. This joust was going to be a combat of minds. With his cabochon reinforcing his psychic powers, he could win a victory.

Setni assumed the shape of a giant eagle and soaring high, attacked the head of the dragon. The chimera at once spat out a stream of fire which singed the eagle's feathers but missed his body.

Setni then changed into a phoenix who plummeted toward his adversary. The dragon, with his fiery breath, reduced him to ashes. Rising again, the phoenix attacked by using a red beam. He lopped off the dragon's arm.

But the dragon resumed his attack, though the flames he belched forth were turned back by the energy field surrounding Setni. The witch then came to the rescue, in the shape of a monster with a pustulous hybrid body, toad and snake. Spitting streams of fetid venom, she flooded the protective field surrounding Setni.

Setni now felt his adversaries were weakening. With a weary gasp, calling upon Wotan, he conjured up a flight of Valkyries. With incandescent swords, they fell upon the two magicians, inflicting deep wounds. Archimago and Duessa flew away, closely pursued by the winged female warriors. Soon, the evil chimeras were only minute dots on the horizon.

Setni, exhausted, slipped to the ground. The magic castle had disappeared. He was in the middle of a green field flecked with flowers. In the distance he could see a woman on a palfrey. The dwarf, perched on his white donkey, followed her. Not far from him, Purple Cross lay in a deep sleep.

Was a battle going to start up again? The knight, thoroughly hoodwinked by Duessa, no longer regarded Setni as a friend: he must avoid a useless fight. Making a final effort, Setni called upon his cabochon to give him back his human form. Exhausted, he fainted.

Chapter III

When the fair Unia suddenly saw three bodies on the ground, she threw herself on Purple Cross lamenting, "Woe! May heaven come to my rescue. I have lost my gentle friend. Without him life is insupportable! I pray God in his mercy to grant me death."

Fortunately, the knight was still very much alive: he was plunged in deep sleep, but the sound of Unia's voice awakened him. "Is that you, light of my life?" he exclaimed, getting to his feet. "Your sorrow fills me with shame! How could I have believed you unfaithful?"

Upon which he took her in his arms. Tears were streaming down Unia's sweet face; she couldn't believe how happy she was after so much sadness.

It was then that the knight noticed the others. He recognized Setni, the friend he had unfairly accused and he lamented his suspicions.

"Gentle sir," he moaned, kneeling beside Setni, "I beseech your forgiveness! Ever since we met, you have been a valiant and loyal friend, rescuing me from pitfalls devised by that devil Archimago and his deadly companion. And I rewarded your kindness by fighting and refusing to believe in your innocence. A lifetime will not be long enough to atone for such a mistake. I shall wear sackcloth and pray for your soul."

Meantime, Setni and the dwarf had also come to. Setni took in the situation at a glance. He had completed his training. Now, the envoy of the Psyborgs had to prove his power by changing his shape. The cabochon quickly carried out his wish; a glance at his clothes showed that he was now wearing a gold-embroidered hauberk. His helmet, resting beside him, was adorned with a princely crown, and the pommel of his sword was encrusted with rubies. He would no longer look to be a poor knight, but a king's son.

He rose and the sun drew flashes from his chiseled silver armor. The body of his former incarnation as Azure Cross seemed to dissolve into thin air. "Lord! This is wondrous!" Purple Cross exclaimed, looking at the newcomer with astonishment. "Who may you be, noble Lord, to wield such enchantment?"

"I am Prince Arthur and I have come straight from fairyland. The knight, Azure Cross, was my faithful servant. He fought the despicable Archimago to the best of his ability. He has gone to an enchanted land, where he will finish his life enjoying eternal felicity. The Queen of the Fairies commissioned me to take his place and put an end to the diabolical sorcerers who are persecuting you. Soon my forces will battle them in their distant hideaway, but I want to help you set free the parents of the woman you love."

"Thanks for your kindness, valorous Prince! Azure Cross had won our hearts; he was a true friend to me. However, my heart aches at the thought that I cannot ask his forgiveness for my offenses."

"Be not troubled! I grant you pardon in his name. Let us go, my friend. Remember you have a difficult mission to accomplish."

With these words, Prince Arthur blew into an ivory oliphant and a magnificent charger galloped up. His scarlet trappings trailed almost to the ground. His pommel and cantle were made of finely chiseled silver and his saddle was covered with ermine. Purple Cross was proud to ride with a knight so splendidly caparisoned.

All four set off on their quest; the two noble lords riding on either side of the lady and the dwarf, on his donkey, bringing up the rear. They rode for a long time.

Setni as Arthur conversed with Unia, while Purple Cross, overcome with remorse, didn't utter a word. Soon night fell and the travelers found shelter in a black grotto called Despair. Around it, rotting stumps clung to faults in the rock. Countless white skeletons covered the ground. Owls, the only birds nesting in this awful place, emitted sinister hoots.

Despite the frightful look of the place, the exhausted travelers settled down in the cavern after having swept aside scattered bones. Purple Cross and Unia stretched out side by side, while Prince Arthur and the dwarf sat down in front of the entrance. They nibbled unenthusiastically at some smoked pork and bread, slaking their thirst with water from a nearby stream. Then fatigue overcame them and they slept.

This time, however, Setni remained alert, his recent victory having given him confidence in his psychic powers. These enabled him to observe the visions which haunted his Purple Cross, without himself being threatened. So he saw a narrow scroll spring up from the cavern floor, twist like a snake, wind up in tight coils and then begin to materialize as human form.

All around, smothered groans and lamentations echoed against the rocky walls as if damned souls, imprisoned in the stone, were murmuring supplications. An evil being gradually became perceptible, surrounded by a dim mist containing blurred forms: one figure had hands folded in supplication, another showed a livid, tear-streaked face of despair; still another was a woman kneeling by a tomb, praying for a restless soul.

This ghostly procession dispersed as the horrible old man became visible. Setni could clearly see the miserable creature crouching near sweaty rocks. He was leaning over Purple Cross. His disheveled gray locks partly hid his fleshless face. His skeletal body was wrapped in filthy, tattered rags held at the waist by a rope. His deep sunk eyes stared blankly into the dark as he chanted in a monotone:

"Poor mortal, you know that everyone's destiny

is woven by the Fates. Those who do not deserve to live must die. Such is the immutable law of the universe. You were unable to appreciate the noble friendship Azure Cross gave you; in return you gave him only ingratitude. Worse, a woman loved you and you cruelly left her to the mercy of tormentors. So why cling to a wretched life, take the step that will give you eternal peace. You have already gone astray many times, why keep up a vain struggle? Take your trusty sword and sever the tenuous thread that binds you to suffering. It was your fault that Azure Cross perished. How could you marry chaste Unia after having given yourself to the wanton Duessa? Come, Knight, die quickly! Death cures all ills."

Setni could see that his companion was affected by this insidious speech. His hand tightened on the hilt of his sword. Torn by anguish, the knight could see no other way out of his situation. He would never succeed in freeing Unia's parents, his one hope for atonement. His soul thirsted to be free of pain.

Feeling dreadfully alone, friendless, loveless, he came to believe in his own iniquity: his hand hesitantly drew the sword from its scabbard. Insidious and persuasive, the evil spirit whispered in his ear: "The longer you drag out your life, the more sins you commit, the more you will have to expiate. Come, Purple Cross, come . . . Atone for your sins . . ."

Hypnotized, the knight leapt up, sweat pouring from his face, his haggard eyes on his gleaming, sharp blade. He stared at it for a moment, then, turning the point toward his breast and opening up his coat of mail, exposed his bare chest.

Setni had seen enough. He could not leave the knight in the clutches of this devil. With all his mental strength, multiplied tenfold by the Psyborgs' cabochon, he concentrated on routing the poisons polluting the mind of Purple Cross.

His steady concentration slowly repulsed the evil spirit; the fleshless ghost melted. Setni then conjured up a vision of Azure Cross who smilingly stretched out both hands:

"Noble friend, do not despair! I am not dead. Prince Arthur entrusted me with a mission which I have accomplished. Now, my Prince is himself going to carry on the fight against Archimago and Duessa. My power would never have been sufficient to conquer them. Trust him as you trusted me! You're a soldier and you know that you cannot abandon a post without an order. You have never retreated before an enemy: you must fight the ghastly chimera who is keeping your Unia's parents captive. You are their only hope. Unia loves you and is awaiting their liberation, then she will plight herself to you. Look, she also begs you not to abandon her."

Thereupon the noble lady appeared to throw herself at the feet of Purple Cross, pleading that he not break his promise and swearing to be his forever. This brought the knight from his dream back to reality; he lifted Unia up and murmured tenderly to her. Then helping her lie down again, he chastely kissed her on the brow. His face shining with serenity, he stretched out on his own pallet, his hands relaxed on the cross formed by the pommel of his sword.

Setni sighed deeply: he had once more succeeded in foiling the insidious magicians, he was gaining ground. He remained on guard for the rest of the night, ready to intervene in case there was a renewed psychic attack, but nothing happened. The respite enabled him to take stock of his situation.

When he had arrived on the planet, his psychic control was not sufficiently strong to fight against creatures who scoffed at material arms and used only the power of suggestion. They were experts in telekinesthesy, telepsychics and hypnosis. They had mocked him as Azure Cross, who understood nothing about what was happening to him.

But now, by his metamorphosis into a prince, he had proven to his friends and enemies his complete control over his body. He could easily wipe out his adversaries' materializations: the destruction of Duessa's castle must surely have surprised them. The perfidious couple had to flee before a man who at first had been putty in their hands. Until now, he had had to accept the false images of this world that were forced upon him. Reality was surely a very different thing. The sudden appearance of this planet in the center of the Milky Way was proof that it had been entirely created by Archimago and Duessa. Unless they had moved it from one point in the universe to another. Or was this star and its inhabitants merely a figment of the imagination?

The Psyborgs must know. Only, they refused to intervene directly. A pity..."

Setni stretched and went on thinking: All these adventures will give the Great Brains of Kalapol something to think about! That, of course, assumes that I shall be soon able to tell them about my tribulations. Oh well! The battle will have to continue so as to throw off balance an opposition ruled solely by psychic forces. Yet, the old rules of strategy still hold: after passive resistance, attack. Hell, the prince is considerably more powerful than Azure Cross. On the other hand, I must not overestimate my strength. The power of the *Psy* amplifier in the cabochon is limited. If the two magicians have a similar gadget, they may outclass me. Therefore, I must watch the reactions of my foes. Before I do anything else, I must set free Unia's parents. When that is done, I can take the offensive on a somewhat different level.

Setni yawned deeply. It had been a long night, but he did not feel too tired. His precious cabochon was both a mental and physical comfort, with it he felt able to meet the trials of another day. His companions were still asleep, so he concentrated on Unia's parents. A vision rose before his eyes: the unfortunate couple were chained to a rock in a deep gorge.

Setni was easily able to locate it: it was half a day's ride to the east. However, the last part of the journey was difficult because they would have to leave the horses behind and continue on foot.

A cerberus that guarded the entrance to the can-

THE ENCHANTED PLANET 55

yon was another of those strange monsters conjured up by the two fiends who ruled this planet. Its scaly talons were like some carnosaur, whereas its hybrid head was that of a mastodon with a trunk and several rows of fangs. It was an enemy to be reckoned with, both because of its dental structure and the corrosive venom it sprayed through its powerful trunk.

The sun had risen and the day would be as beautiful as the preceding ones. It suddenly struck Setni that it had not rained once since his arrival, yet streams and rivers flowed free and full. This improbability merely highlighted the wild ecology of this continent and was further proof of its artificiality.

A few clouds lingering in the sky were like large golden discs. Ribbons of fog lent a sinister aspect to the clearing. Every stump looked like a guardian monster waiting to attack travelers. Actually, there seemed to be no real danger. Setni therefore awakened his companions who had no recollection of their hideous nightmares. They all partook of a frugal meal, looking forward to better fare at their next one.

When they were ready to leave, Prince Arthur thought he should tell his Purple Cross what to expect. "Noble knight, rejoice. Your quest is drawing to an end. I have seen, by magic, where your beloved's parents are imprisoned. We should reach there when the sun is at its zenith. However, I must warn you that your task will not be easy."

"Noble knight, you gladden my heart! Have our trials really come to an end?"

"I swear to you by all I hold most sacred: before the day is done you will have given your beloved proof of your valor."

"I know that I can trust you, noble Arthur. The combat will surely be a fierce one. I want, before doing anything, to make a vow. By all that is holy, I swear to serve you faithfully for three years, if our Lord grant me life after this deadly combat. This will be a token of the gratitude I owe your Knight of the Azure Cross, and also for all you have done for me. Last night I think you came to my defense, but I have only a confused recollection of that dream."

"It was nothing, friend! However, I deeply appreciate your vow and thank you for it."

Then the valiant knights spurred their horses forward to a trot. Unia and the dwarf followed, exchanging worried remarks. The landscape was different from the cheerful countryside through which they had ridden before. All around there were untidy piles of rocks, the result of errosion. They formed fanciful shapes: a dog's head, a warrior's hieratric profile; delicate, lacy, convoluted stones. Most of the rocks had blood-colored veins as though they had been scattered by a wounded dragon. The horses reluctantly followed the narrow path winding between steep bluffs. Only sparse vegetation survived in this arid locale.

Setni paid no attention to the landscape, not even wondering what mysterious reality was hidden by this frightening scenery. His sole concern was to reach their destination as quickly as possible and to help Purple Cross set free the two captives. What was the role of Unia's parents in this tangle? Doubtless all these characters played a part in the strange allegory of this abnormal world.

Purple Cross was anxiously contemplating the decisive battle that lay ahead. The end of his quest meant that Unia would be his at last. He frequently glanced at the lady of his heart, drawing strength and comfort from her.

She did her best to hide her own anxiety. But she wondered with trepidation whether Purple Cross would succeed against such enemies. Fortunately, Prince Arthur could come to the rescue if need be: he had given proof of his powers and surely would not be only a spectator at a fight between his friend and the captor of the old couple. Yet, poor Unia was so upset at times that tears came to her large eyes. She had to make a superhuman effort to smile at Purple Cross when he looked at her.

The path which they followed was becoming steeper and the horses often stumbled on loose stones. The riders had to give careful guidance to their mounts, for they were now skirting a deep valley; one false step could be fatal.

As far as the eye could see, there were only bare promontory whose peaks disappeared in a bluish mist. It was a dead landscape, no vegetation. The presence of the dragon seemed to have wiped out all traces of life in this corner of the world. An occasional cliff shaped like old ruins gave the impression that there once had been a castle on these wild heights. Seen up close, however, they revealed stones that had been shaped by nature alone.

For the time being, the two evil magicians seemed uninterested in the little group: no images, no vibrations, were perceptible to Setni's sharpened senses. Apparently Archimago and Duessa were using all their psychic strength to support the monster they had conjured up. This was rather reassuring to Setni: these damned sorcerers were doubtless beginning to have some respect for him.

Soon the path plunged into a narrow crevasse, hewn in the sheer rock. It meandered along the side of the bluff, affording a view of the entire canyon. The horses kept their footing with increasing difficulty; finally the riders were obliged to dismount and continue on foot, holding the bridles. It was at a bend in the path on the rocks that the two knights caught sight of their alarming goal.

The fearful appearance of the monster, larger than two horses put together, sent shivers down their spines. The armored head bore a jagged crest and on either side, two large pendulous eyes oscillated constantly. Its body, covered with a thick scally armor, rested on four powerful taloned feet. But the worst was that the infernal monster spouted through its trunk a venomous saliva that broke with a roar on the rocks, which corroded in billows of smoke. The beast's bifurcated tongue then darted out to lick up the scum which streamed out of the rock, then repeated the whole process.

Behind the monster, bound to two prismatic

crystals, two helpless old people suffered the tortures of the damned. It was plain, from their skeletal thinness, that they had been without food. Their heads hung down to their chests, they had lost all hope and no strength even to complain.

At the sight of them, the Knight of the Purple Cross furiously rushed at their tormentor. He unsheathed his sword and, covering himself with his shield, rushed to the bottom of the revine.

Prince Arthur followed close behind, his mind prepared to ward off any psychic attack from the magicians. He could probably have repelled this fantastic image as easily as he had the visions of the night before, but he preferred to leave the initiative to his adversaries.

Purple Cross had reached the bottom of the gorge. Standing squarely, he waited for the monster to lunge.

It was pawing the ground enraged, staring with bloodshot eyes at the foolhardy man who dared to challenge him. Then he charged forward heavily, like bull.

When he reached the knight, he viciously spat out two streams of venom on the knight's shield. The metal began to bubble and sizzle; so great was the corrosive power that the buckler was pierced in several places. Purple Cross made a feint, then struck a mighty blow to the hideous head. His sword glanced off the bony crest but severed one of the eyes, which rolled in the dust. The monster let out a howl of pain and took off at top speed on his stumpy legs. A purulent puss spurted from his wound, sizzling as it fell on the ground.

The knight had apparently won the first round, but Prince Arthur did not relax his vigilance. Their foe was by no means put out of action. Maddened with pain, he executed an extraordinarily rapid about-face for so heavy a creature and hurled himself on his diminutive challenger. Once more he spurted forth venom. This time, the perforated shield could stop only a portion of the venom; the rest splashed against the knight's armor which also began to sizzle. Blinded by the deadly fumes, Purple Cross was unable to dodge the charge. He struck at the snout, cutting off the bifurcated tongue, but he slipped in the puss that covered the ground and fell, dropping his shield.

The monster, with deafening roars, closed in. Nothing, it seemed, could save the poor knight. Unia whimpered with fear and covered her eyes with trembling hands. But the envoy from the Psyborgs was watching; his mental energy, strengthened by the cabochon, caused an invisible wall to rise. The dragon crashed into it with a horrible noise.

Stunned and dizzy, the monster staggered back. What possible obstacle could keep his victim out of reach, just when the puny worm appeared defeated? Meantime, the knight pulled himself together and boldly marched forward, sword in hand.

The domestic beast then changed itself into a hippogryph and, flapping its wings, soared upward; then hovering over the knight, threatened him with

THE ENCHANTED PLANET

its talons. The latter, whirling his sword about his head, managed to cut off one of the feet, throwing the monster off balance. It then struck at Purple Cross with its sharp beak, almost knocking him unconscious.

At that point, Prince Arthur enveloped the combatants in thick darkness. This gave Purple Cross a chance to recover. Then Arthur dissipated the inky mists and the sun shone again over the fighting terrain. The hippogryph rose up once more; plummeting beak foremost, he prepared to smash his enemy's skull.

The knight held his ground, then quickly sidestepped. The chimera, unable to change course, fell heavily. With a quick stroke of his sword, Purple Cross cut off one of its wings. The creature instantly became a seven-headed hydra, vomiting fire through each mouth. The knight, choking, fell down on one knee; his armor, instead of protecting him, was hot as an oven.

This time, the end seemed inevitable. But Arthur was on guard. A black cloud materialized over the opponents and torrents of rain fell as the hydra, struck by lightning, collapsed, howling with pain. Purple Cross, taking advantage of this disaster, sliced off each hideous head. Then, exhausted, he slipped quietly to the ground next to the dead monster.

Without transition, the arid canyon was transformed into a sunny, rolling valley. A castle surrounded by a moat of limpid water appeared. A merry little procession was crossing the drawbridge, led by two noble, silver-haired persons. Musicians and pages clad in crimson velvet followed. Unia, crowned with asphodel, rosy with pleasure, walked behind.

The Knight of the Purple Cross stood next to the prince, watching their approach. He felt awkward in his rusty, dented armor and could not believe his eyes. The procession stopped before the two knights; Unia's father, taking her delicate hand, placed it on the rough gauntlet of the Knight of the Purple Cross. The knight knelt down to receive the blessing of Unia's parents, whom he had restored to normal life.

Chapter IV

The knights' quest had been successful. During the ensuing days, the servants readied the banquet to celebrate the betrothal of Unia and Purple Cross.

For the first time since landing on this strange planet, Setni felt that he was living in a normal world. The girl's parents behaved like ordinary mortals did in the Confederation: they were extremely pleased at having so brave a knight for their future son-in-law. They made the guests' stay as pleasant as possible. Setni had a comfortable room overlooking the castle moat. From his window, he could admire the beauty of the scenery.

Purple Cross and Unia took long walks in the surrounding countryside; they appeared to be very happy and spent their entire days together. In the evening, everyone gathered in the large hall where a wood fire burned in a fireplace surmounted by the family coat-of-arms. Everyone was happy to chat, listen to a minstrel and watch a juggler.

Everything seemed so calm and so real that Setni began to wonder if he was hallucinating. Was this world really controlled by Archimago and Duessa?

There had been no further sign of them; they seemed to have forgotten the *psy* powers of Prince Arthur. Nevertheless, Setni remained on guard. Sometimes, when he was leaning out of his window to see the castle's reflection in the waters of the moat, he would test the power of his cabochon. Then the landscape would alter completely.

Instead of the green countryside, he would see only arid hills beneath the burning rays of the local sun. All trace of life would vanish and Setni, puzzled, could not tell which world was the real one.

One week after the death of the dragon, the betrothal ceremony took place. Messengers had carried invitations and countless knights and noble ladies clad in festive raiment arrived at the castle. Prince Arthur was in the reception line in the hall, welcoming the guests as they arrived. He scanned each face, trying to spot his foes among them, but the two magicians had not come to the feast.

The guests sat around a huge trestle table, talking cheerfully, and the cup bearers began to fill the vermeil goblets. As was the custom on that planet, no one had to cook dishes nor draw wine from casks.

Each guest had only to wish and the crystal decanters were filled with ruby or amber-colored wine; platters covered with venison, dressed roasts, or silvery fish appeared. They all helped themselves lavishly. These people's years were brief, but they lived in abundance without worrying about the morrow. That situation many Polluxians might have envied. The Knight of the Purple Cross held

Unia's hand in his; wreathed in smiles, they were blissfully happy.

When the last sweetmeats had been consumed, Unia's father stood up to request silence. He said: "My Lords and Ladies, you have been invited to this feast to hear happy tidings: Unia, our only daughter, has decided, with our full consent, to plight her troth to the valiant Knight of the Purple Cross. So great is his fame that our daughter's choice fills us with joy and we accept him as our son-in-law. But we are also indebted to him for a service we can never repay. Victims of evil spells, we had been reduced to a pitiable state: prisoners of an infernal monster and stripped of all possessions, we awaited death as a deliverance. But we had forgotten the loyalty and courage of the noble knight whom we now welcome into our family. With valor, he was not afraid to face the demonic dragon who held us. The Knight of the Purple Cross killed him after a bitter fight, breaking the spells that had been cast over us. What could be more fitting, therefore, than our giving to him our loving Unia. Hear ye then, my Lords and Ladies, our daughter is promised in marriage to the man of her choice. In three years from today, the ceremony to unite them forever will take place." The guests rose in unison, toasting and congratulating the future bride and bridegroom.

Then the elderly knight continued: "You are no doubt wondering why they wait so long. My future son-in-law will tell you."

The Knight of the Purple Cross stood up and,

turning to Prince Arthur, said with emotion: "Noble friends, you will readily understand my reason for putting off the wedding. Without Prince Arthur, I could never have carried out my quest, Thanks to his help, to his magic powers, I was able to slay the accursed chimera who tortured the noble parents of my beloved. In the course of my long quest, he never failed to be of help and brotherly support. He sent me a valiant, noble companion, the Knight of the Azure Cross, who was by my side for a long time. That is why I took a solemn vow to spend three years in the service of the Prince, if he is willing."

Arthur replied at once: "Dear friend, it would be churlish of me to reject such an offer. I accept gratefully, but your help will be needed for only as long as my quest. When I have accomplished it, you will be free to marry the adorable Unia."

Again, the rafters rang with the acclamations of the guests. Then the musicians played and Unia's father opened the ball, dancing with his daughter. The Knight of the Purple Cross then took his place and the ball continued, until late into the night.

The old gentleman, seeing Prince Arthur alone, went up to him. "Sir Knight," he whispered in his ear, "I won't forget how much I owe you, so I shall tell you something I believe will be helpful in carrying out your mission. The two sorcerers whom you are pursuing cast their spell on me because I have a secret they want to keep from you. You have proven your valor and your strength of mind; you have withstood the trials and tribulations imposed upon you.

"That is why I can tell you where your quarry has gone to ground. Your trials are not over. Find the magic mirror; in its reflection of an enchanted lake, you will see the hiding place of our oppressors who have condemned us to lead an artificial existence that violates natural laws. At the very bottom of that lake is an invisible city. If you reach it, you will understand the reality of this world. You will have to fight alone; your companion will help you only by his friendship. You will have to struggle against powerful spells, but if you are victorious, you will discover truth. I can say no more. Know that we are behind you with all our hearts. Your victory will free us forever from the painful state into which we have been plunged by those two evil creatures who are enemies of humankind."

Setni tried to thank the wise old man, but the latter slipped away. Setni was left to his thoughts. So his suppositions were confirmed.

These ladies with their hennins and beautiful robes, these knights in velvet doublets, were no more than actors in a vast drama mounted to test his psychic strength. Unlike the Psyborgs who had created an illusory civilization for their sole entertainment, Archimago and Duessa had created this world in order to test him. Why?

It was obvious that his tribulations as Prince Arthur would increase and were leading toward a secret goal. Fortunately, his brain had become more powerful and there seemed to be no limit to the powers of the cabochon. Yet, in spite of himself, Setni identified with the puppets with whom he lived: they seemed as human as he.

After the ceremony, when the guests had left, life in the castle returned to normal. Purple Cross and Unia were so happy that Setni hadn't the heart to continue his mission immediately. To pass the time, he decided to make a few experiments.

He knew that on this planet there were strange natural laws totally different from those of the Confederation. The astronaut built a number of simple mechanical devices. Perhaps the Psyborgs were wrong in assuming that Polluxian instruments and weapons were useless here. First, he made a simple winch, then a block and tackle built on the principle of a lever. Neither worked. Intrigued, Setni built a water clock, hoping to be able to measure time on this clockless planet. The gadget was quite useless.

Stung, he made one last attempt: he tried to make a hot air balloon. The balloon is held aloft by the difference of density between the temperature of air inside the balloon and that of the air outside. For several days, to the astonishment of his hosts, he sewed fine silk hangings together, waterproofing them with resin. It was highly inflammable, impracticable for human passengers.

With infinite patience, the ingenious Setni succeeded: burning straw supplied the warm air. The experiment took place in the castle courtyard. Everyone wondered if the Prince had become mad. At first, everything went naturally: the huge sphere expanded, rose a few feet, tugging at its suspension lines. The reed basket even left the ground. But, after a few seconds, with no apparent tear in the material, the majestic balloon collapsed onto the fire. It burned in a flash, leaving only ashes.

This was final proof: the Psyborgs were right. This world was ruled by evil forces. Did everything undergo unpredictable changes, or was it all unreal? The only way of learning more was to find the mirror of which Unia's father had spoken.

The Prince and the Knight of the Purple Cross left the castle one sunny morning. For a long time they could see Unia, silhouetted against the towers, waving a kerchief in farewell. Then she disappeared in the morning mist and the two knights silently rode for a long time, meeting no one. Setni knew that the magic mirror was hidden in a deep grotto, located on an island in the middle of a lake, two days' ride northward.

He labored under no illusions: the magicians would not allow him to reach his goal without presenting him with new obstacles. He was very much on his guard, but nothing seemed to occur. This worried the envoy of the Psyborgs. What would really happen if such conditions extended to all inhabited planets? It would be catastrophic for the Confederation. Every mechanical device would stop functioning, even airships would be unusable. Perhaps this was what the Psyborgs hoped to avert? What a responsibility rested on his shoulders!

His gloomy meditation was interrupted. They were riding on a narrow path that led to the bottom of a valley. When he reached it, he was startled to discover a river that was flowing back toward its source.

"Noble friend!" Arthur exclaimed. "This is wondrous. Is this the way bodies of water flow in your country?"

"What's so surprising about that?" answered Purple Cross. "Rivers flow to and from their source. It almost never rains here, because the oceans would overflow."

Setni made no comment about this strange new aspect of the world in which he now lived as Arthur. The rulers of this planet were expert manipulators, just like the Psyborgs. He would have to be doubly on guard. Just then, a pleasant island appeared in the midst of the river. A bridge covered with beautiful flowers led to it. On its green lawns, couples crowned with garlands of flowers sang merry tunes as they danced gaily to the music of invisible instruments.

"Valiant Prince," the Knight of the Purple Cross warned him with a shudder, "this accursed place is the Isle of Idleness, with the Grove of Delights in the center. Would it not be madness to set foot here?"

Before replying, Setni consulted his trusty cabochon. This enabled him to see through to the heart of the mirage. He scanned the Eden-like Grove of Delights and saw in the center of it, a Cyclopean edifice made of green basalt blocks. From a black portico, a winding staircase led underground. Hieroglyphics adorned the facade of the porch. At the bottom, a dazzling light shone. Priceless treasures were there, among them the mirror that would show him the hideout of the masters of this planet. His mind encountered an impenetrable aura and was unable to probe further. He would have to go to the hiding place of the mirror.

"Dear friend, it grieves me to leave you," he said to Purple Cross. "I must get the magic mirror. You must stay here while I go to that island. However, to make sure you will be safe during my absence, I am going to give you protection against the spells of Archimago and his companion."

Setni was purposely making a decisive experiment. Would he be able to mentally bring forth a whole company of brave knights? Everything went smoothly, a cloud of dust appeared on the horizon. Pennons bearing the emblem of the Azure Cross appeared and finally, thirty or so knights lined up before Prince Arthur.

"Here is a noble company," exclaimed the Purple Cross. "I shall have nothing to fear. These valiant warriors could fight a legion of dragons."

"Friend, you will be under their protection while I am on that island. I may be gone a long time; don't become impatient. No harm can befall you. If they should disappear, return to Unia's castle without waiting, for that would mean something has happened to me."

"I should be ashamed to leave you thus! I would go to the very jaws of hell to help you," Purple Cross cried.

"Don't take on something you cannot handle, dear friend. That will be your ultimate service to me. The power of the two sorcerers is such that you cannot face them alone; therefore, swear to obey me. I should like someone to know what has happened, should any one come to enquire of me."

The knight gave his word, reluctantly. If Prince Arthur's magic failed him, Purple Cross would be in no position to rescue him. Setni made a gesture of farewell and, without a backward glance, rode onto the bridge leading to the Isle of Idleness.

He had never seen a more attractive scene. Flowering trees were reflected in the emerald water. Streams meandered gently amid alabaster gazebos; small classical rotundas were reflected in crystal clear waters. Aquatic plants floated between the peaceful banks. Vines wound around mossy tree trunks to the tops of the foliage, forming arches.

There were pleasant scents in the air: the perfume of the many flowers dotting the green lawns. However, there was an aura of unreality about this idyllic place. Perhaps it was the absence of birds and animals.

The couples on the island seemed completely happy. Some, holding hands, rambled along humming melodies; others embraced tenderly, others quite unashamedly made love. A fountain of wine flowed in the center of the belvedere and heaps of succulent food were everywhere.

Prince Arthur, impervious to the lures of laughing nymphs who clung to his stirrups, headed straight for the center of the island. When he reached the Grove of Delights he saw, in a ray of sunlight, an adorable creature with limpid eyes, her long diaphanous veils floating in the breeze.

His heart skipped a beat as he recognized the person he loved most in the world, the lovely Nicolette. But Setni knew that this was only a ruse to turn him from his goal. Yet, the effect of this apparition was so great that he was unable to repulse it. At times she appeared to dissolve in a light mist; a moment later, her dazzling smile reappeared.

With her arms outstretched, the dryad invited the knight to follow her. Her rosy lips murmured his name. Setni, defeated, pulled his horse to a halt in the middle of the field. The knight dropped his reins, took his right foot out of its stirrup and prepared to dismount.

Just then, his hand brushed against the cabochon on his belt. The vision dissolved instantly; instead of Nicolette, he saw Duessa the witch. Her long black hair streaked her cadaverous skin and a skeletal grin was on her face. The cheerful landscape had likewise been transformed; he saw only a ramshackle stone wall surmounted by a dark building covered with hieroglyphics.

Spurring his charger on, Setni climbed the steep slope. Stumbling on fallen stones, his horse pushed on. It seemed to Setni now that the walls were part of some ruins where the inhabitants had died under evil spells.

The portico he had seen appeared before him in all its terrible majesty. Between two pilasters covered with demonic carvings, a dark staircase plunged into the heart of the rock. At the bottom, he could see the heap of treasures whose provenance was lost in the night of time. Setni dismounted and, unsheathing his sword, slowly penetrated the sinister gloom.

Chapter V

His descent seemed interminable. His steel shoes echoed on the stairs; he automatically counted the steps as he peered into the darkness ahead. The luminous dot below slowly grew larger. After the hundredth step, the blue square of the sky disappeared behind him. A pungent smell of mildew was almost unbearable, but that was less terrible than the tempting visions that assailed him.

At times it was Nicolette, who begged him to give up this undertaking. Then it was Huon, who urged him to turn back; sometimes Pentoser joined the phantasms of his subconscious. Setni, his hand on his cabochon, managed to disperse them, but as he neared his goal, the visions became more insistent.

It seemed to him that imprecise shapes flitted about him. Huge bats brushed their hairy wings against him, changing into hideous vampires with human faces and long curved fangs, trying to bite him. The knight covered himself with his shield, lowered his head and continued, not allowing himself to be intimidated.

Suddenly he heard a hideous cry: the Knight of the Purple Cross was calling for help. Setni hesitated for a second. Then, shaking his head, he continued his descent. Either the magic knights would succeed in repelling creatures of the two magicians, or else they would collapse. In that case, it would be useless to go to the rescue.

He was now close enough to see the priceless riches piled up in the deep cavern: finely chiseled precious metals, gems of every description, heaps of gold pieces were scattered on the floor. But the faces engraved on the coins, although human, were unfamiliar to him. The coins had been minted in some long-forgotten past, by a people who had disappeared without a trace. Their peaceful look was reminiscent of ancient Terrestrials. The shape of the tankards, cups and bowls was like those used by humans. These beings had developed a powerful civilization and enormous wealth before vanishing for all time.

Setni went down the last step. At that point an evanescent form materialized before his eyes: a hideous old man with a greedy smirk. He wore a dust-stained golden tunic, his skeletal fingers covered with sumptuous rings. He was holding out to Setni a vast sack made of brocade, an invitation to pick up whatever he wanted.

Deep within, a small voice held Setni back. He had always despised wealth; the prospect of an easy, pleasure-filled life did not appeal to him. Gathering up his strength, he repulsed temptation. With a swift gesture, Setni picked up the magic mirror which had brought him to this evil spot. Then, without a backward glance, he ran up the steps, scorning the priceless treasures.

He became winded and had to slow down. Slipping the handle of the mirror into his belt, he concentrated on teleporting to the surface. A few seconds later, Prince Arthur shot out of the Cyclopean porch, flew over the Isle of Idleness and the Grove of Delights. He returned to his starting point. There, he saw a disquieting sight: his magic warriors, in circle around the Knight of the Purple Cross, were fighting off a legion of demonic warriors, each riding a winged Pegasus.

The melee was indescribable: the assailants were flying at great speed, shooting black arrows at the knights; in a quick about-face, they reversed direction and charged again. The shields, pierced with sharp darts, looked like huge porcupines. Almost a third of Prince Arthur's soldiers were wounded.

Setni knew that this was nothing but an illusory battle. However, he realized that a defeat would prove he was powerless to repulse his foes' phantasms. He instantly transformed himself into a winged chimera, spewing long scarlet flames. He was surprised to discover that his psychic power could now rival the magicians' transformations.

Like an eagle dive-bombing its prey, the chimera swooped down upon the black warriors, emitting crimson flames. In the face of this attack, the assailants dispersed. They soon disappeared over the horizon. Setni, resuming his previous shape as Arthur, materialized next to the Knight of the Purple Cross, who could hardly believe his eyes.

"I thank you with all my heart, my Lord!" Purple Cross exclaimed. "Had you not come to my aid, we should all have been cut to pieces. I see now how powerful you are; let Archimago and Duessa beware! Never before has our world seen such a magician! But enough compliments! Is that the mirror you were seeking?"

"Yes, dear friend. I wrested it from a sorcerer who was tempting me with riches. Henceforth, there is nothing to stand in the way of our learning the truth about the strange things that are happening here. Follow me; we must find the lake where the forbidden city is hidden."

The little procession of knights resumed its progress, following the course of the river. The island soon disappeared behind them. The river meandered through a green plain where they saw no living thing. Toward evening, in the distance Setni saw the reflection of the setting sun on a large lake. That was surely the place Unia's father had told him about. He spurred his horse, hoping to reach it before night fall.

When the little troop had reached the banks of the calm water, the sun had set. It was sufficiently light to see that nothing marred its glassy surface. Setni looked at the reflection in the magic mirror. He was disappointed to notice nothing unusual. Small waves lapped the shore of the lake, where clumps of stiff reeds and stretches of aquatic plants lay.

"What do you think, friend?" Setni asked Purple Cross. "Has this mirror lost its magic, or have I been deceived?"

"Well," replied the Knight, frowning. "Perhaps its powers function only in sunlight. We shall have to wait until tomorrow morning to find out. Let us pitch camp here by the shore in a dry spot. Our sentries will forestall any nasty surprises. Now, we'll restore ourselves with a good meal. I am famished."

"Good advice, friend! A rest will do us all good. I'll wager that tomorrow will bring us more adventure. Let's find a good place to camp."

The knights spotted a slight elevation overlooking the lake. There was a splendid, colorful view. Soon, delicious meat roasted on spits appeased the hunger of the travelers.

The only sounds during the night were the periodic calls of sentries. No stranger approached the camp, nor did nightmares disturb the Prince or the Purple Knight. At dawn, just as the water was beginning to reflect the flames of the rising sun, the knights dragged themselves from sleep and ate a frugal breakfast.

Setni was waiting impatiently for the sun to appear fully over the horizon so that he could look into his mirror. Finally, the dazzling sphere shone in all its splendor through the veil of morning mist.

Setni seized the mirror with a hand that shook slightly and, with his back to the lake, studied its reflection. For a moment he couldn't credit his eyes. He called upon his cabochon to repel possible magic-induced images, but the scene remained unchanged.

In the middle of the lake lay a wondrous city. Alabaster buildings in the shape of prisms were silhouetted against the sky. Oddly, none of them had doors or windows, yet this fantastic metropolis teemed with life. Creatures who looked human traveled on long moving belts that wound in and about the city, and up and down the high buildings. Curious triangular machines flew at great speed above all this, occasionally landing on platforms on the tops of towers.

Until then, Setni had assumed that no instrument which operated by the normal laws of physics could function on this planet. Yet this city looked exactly like Kalapol, capital of the Confederation. The flying machines seemed to resemble those of the Polluxians. The rolling belts also obeyed the laws of physics.

What was he to think? Was this a new vision? Archimago and Duessa had conjured up a primitive medieval world. There was perhaps nothing to prevent their conjuring up a civilization with a more sophisticated technology. Yet, Setni had reservations.

He thought to himself. "On this visionary planet, none of the simple machines I built worked. How could my adversaries succeed where I failed? Perhaps this deserted planet was once populated with artificial inhabitants, but previously sheltered a civilization similar to the Confederation. Then the image in the mirror is of an era now past."

Setni decided he'd find out by going into that unreal metropolis. He asked his companion to look into the mirror, then sought his advice. Purple Cross, curious about the magic mirror, quickly complied with the request. Unfortunately, he was unable to understand this strange city such as he had never seen before. He thought the flying machines were large birds and the moving belt gigantic snakes.

Setni did not enlighten him. Resuming his study, he noticed that a paved road starting at the shore of the lake led to the city. Followed by the Knight of the Purple Cross and his retinue, he set forth.

This move obviously annoyed his enemies, for the waters began to boil and a dozen marine monsters attacked the knights, unhorsing some of them. It was a desperate battle. Repulsing the assailants with lances was difficult, for Setni's knights could not pierce the viscous hides of the great reptiles.

Purple Cross changed his tactics; he aimed for the gaping jaws of the monsters who were trying to bite the legs of the chargers. This move was more successful. Soon the carcasses of the monsters covered the surface of the lake and gradually sank to the bottom.

The knights who had been unhorsed were able to get back into their saddles. Shortly, all traces of the monsters had vanished. These creatures had also been materializations of the two magicians.

The column of knights was halfway to the city when Archimago and Duessa attacked again; this time they conjured up marvelous sirens whose lewd songs made Setni's pulse beat. He quickly summoned up images of Nicolette and Unia. Then, the sirens' lures were useless; their naked, seductive breasts left the two friends unmoved. The magic knights were, of course, immune.

They safely reached the middle of the lake. There, the scene changed once again. The road ended on a large island. Thick vegetation covered the ancient ruins which impeded the progress of the horses.

"There must once have been a city here," Purple Cross observed.

"Assuredly! And I am positive these are the remains of the city that looked alive in the mirror," the Prince replied.

"How strange! Seen from the shore, it looked full of life," Purple Cross cried.

"That's because the mirror showed us an image of a distant past. A civilization thrived on this planet, then vanished. Why? Those two wicked sorcerers probably know the answer."

"You think they are responsible for this destruction? It happened a long time ago. Do you think they are immortal?"

"I don't know. Their ancestors could have caused this, unless their magic makes travel through time possible."

"Those are wondrous things of which you speak, hard for me to understand. However, if magic is required, you will soon be able to work it!"

"An examination of these ruins should tell me a great deal. You will pitch camp here and wait for me, with my knights. They have given proof of their courage: you have nothing to fear from Archimago and Duessa. Don't worry if I am gone overly long; it will take me time to study the remains of this city. Rest assured, I shall do everything in my power to rid you of the sorcerers who oppress you. Trust me."

Saying which, Setni dismounted and walked amid the majestic ruins, the remains of the towers he had seen in the mirror. Close inspection of the massive foundations showed them to be perfectly smooth, free from unevenness. The diameter of each tower was roughly a hundred yards; its walls, at the bottom, were as thick as the length of a horse.

The tops of the building were smooth, as if they had been neatly decapitated by a gigantic saber. There was no debris on the ground, only a thick coat of rubble. Sparse vines clung to the pulverized glass.

All this seemed to indicate use of a nuclear weapon in war, some super-atomic disintegrator. Was this proof that normal laws of physics had once functioned on this planet? Setni was sure he was right. After poking about the ruins without finding a single entrance, Setni had recourse to his cabochon. He regretted not having a cavity detector. His piercing eyes, strengthened by the cabochon, led him to his goal: a huge hypogeum deep in the rock.

His next step was to find the entrance. Setni teleported himself to the remains of a tower. From there he spotted a circular well, partially hidden by shrubbery.

It was an anti-G well once used by the tenants of the building to reach various floors. It was easy to spot the landings, by regularly spaced markings on the walls. The machinery no longer worked, but this was proof positive that there had existed on this star a normal civilization.

So the mirror *had* shown a picture of the past, long before the city had vanished. He could only hope that these people had concealed in the hypogeum some record of their origins.

Setni let himself gently down the bottomless cylinder. His compatriots would have been surprised to see his powers of telekinesis. Setni felt at ease using his psychic powers. He now brought these into play instinctively.

His descent was rapid; his feet soon touched the thick dust at the bottom of the well. The last doors were blocked by heaps of dust. Setni singled out the door next to the large underground passages he had noticed from the tower. He cautiously entered them, on the alert for a sudden attack.

He was getting tired of wearing his heavy armor; with relief he again wore his space suit, but he kept the precious belt with the cabochon. He continued his explorations. No footprints were visible on the dust. No one had visited the site since the catastrophe.

He now entered the marvelous hypogeum. The beams of his flashlight barely reached the high ceiling covered with frescoes which were remarkably preserved. They depicted scenes in the lives of vanished people.

Between the huge pillars that supported the vault there were statues of dead rulers who, seated on high thrones, had preserved in their hierarctic pose the majesty of their former status. Setni proceeded to the other end of the hall.

Between the two columns of a portico, he saw a bronze door covered with bas-reliefs. Setni recognized the allegories of various branches of science: physics, chemistry, biology, astronomy, philosophy; further proof of the similarity to his civilization, but it still gave no clue as to its origin nor age. The frescoes, the nameless statues, could have been the work of any people in the Galaxy. Perhaps the clue lay beyond the heavy door.

Setni tried to understand how it opened. The door fitted very closely into the jamb. By concentrating with his mind, Setni figured out that the lock was a mechanism which controlled a simple latch. He opened the latch by using telekinesis.

He opened the door by tugging at one of its decorations. It swung squeakily on its hinges, revealing a dark staircase descending into the rock below. The opening had been so thoroughly sealed that there was not a speck of dust. The steps were as clean as when the last scientist of this race had walked on them.

Before venturing down the steps Setni prudently made a psychic probe. Everytime he used his *psy* faculties he felt exhausted, but he recovered quickly. The staircase contained no trap and led directly to a second room, the size of the one he had just left.

Unlike the first, there were no frescoes nor statues; it was a laboratory equipped with countless instruments, all in excellent condition, set out in parallel rows.

Setni thought of those scientists, a millennia ago, who had so carefully stored their scientific gear to preserve them from the cataclysm that was to swallow them. What had their lives been like? Their hopes? How could they have disappeared so completely, possessing as they did such technical knowledge?

Consumed with curiosity, Setni went down the steps four at a time. The laboratory corresponded exactly to the vision he had seen. The rectangular apparatuses, which were about waist high, appeared to be intact and, incredibly, were functioning.

The astronaut was baffled by what he saw through the transparent covers of the machines. Diamond particles, in constant motion, formed ever-changing shapes and created miniature constellations.

Every time he approached one of the mysterious instruments the particles whirled about madly. Setni could not figure out how these machines detected the presence of humans. Continuing his investigation, he came to a sort of throne in the middle of the room.

Setni was more and more puzzled. Ought he to sit on it? Was this another trap? These machines were produced by a technology similar to that of the Polluxians. However, they did not work by psychic means, for he received no message from them, and his efforts to use telekinesis failed. Obviously, these installations had been set up by people entirely different from Archimago and Duessa, who had done their best to keep him from getting here.

The throne was awaiting an intelligent creature to sit in it. Why not try? After all, the cabochon continued to protect him. If it was a trap, it couldn't be any worse than the ones from which he had extricated himself before.

Setni made one final psychic probe of his surroundings. There appeared to be nothing threatening. He circled the throne, examining its every joint, unable to detect anything sinister. Once he sat down on the chair, which was quite comfortable, nothing occurred. The astronaut smiled as he realized how nervous he was; after all, this chair had probably been used by some scientist lecturing his students.

He hadn't time to give it any thought: thin fluorescent plasma filaments streaked out of each machine, straight toward his head. Conscious of having stupidly been trapped, Setni made a desperate effort to escape. His muscles refused to obey.

He was conscious of the tenuous threads moving toward him, lashing at his brain, penetrating deep into his neurons. He was overcome by a hideous migraine; nausea shook him. Then he realized his hands had become luminescent, then translucent. A black veil passed over his eyes and he lost consciousness.

Chapter VI

When Setni opened his eyes, he realized that he had been transported into an unknown world. Lost in the darkness, the astronaut looked up at a sky studded with unfamiliar constellations. What portion of space-time had he crossed, propelled by the powerful machines of the hypogeum? What unmeasurable distance had he crossed?

This time his cabochon had been powerless to protect him, but he was certain that Archimago and Duessa had nothing to do with this. This technology was so dissimilar from their purely psychic methods. He had now left that strange planet, but where had he gone? The power that had transported him through the universe was far mightier than any Polluxian science or the Psyborgs.

He shivered in the cool night air. Cut off from those he loved, he felt lost, as helpless as a child. Despairing for a moment, he was tempted to lie down in the prickly grass and die. He was a wretched exile in a lost corner of the universe.

Suddenly a thin cloud veiled the stars and, with a gentle hum, a triangular flying object landed before

Setni. The door of the cockpit opened, showing him a cushioned seat in front of a transparent windshield.

Setni thought: this open invitation boded no good. But after a second's pause, he shrugged, stepped into the craft and sat down. Those who had projected him amid the stars must have powerful means. He might as well become acquainted with their intentions. If they had a technology comparable to his compatriots', his psychic power gave him a considerable advantage: better try his luck than to flee aimlessly on an unknown planet, hunted by people who were remarkable.

The lightweight craft was operated by an efficient remote control system: he had scarcely sat down when the door closed and the propellers started. The craft flew over a chain of mountains at high speed, then went straight toward a dim light flickering on the horizon. The light soon grew brighter and the astronaut saw a marvelous city which looked exactly like the one he had glimpsed in the magic mirror.

A few seconds later, the craft landed on a platform located on the side of a huge prismatic building. The door opened, Setni got out, and found himself in the presence of three persons whose costumes looked familiar. There were two men and one beautiful woman.

One of the men bowed in welcome. When he straightened up, Setni almost cried out in surprise. There stood the Knight of the Purple Cross. The resemblance was striking. However, his clothes were

THE ENCHANTED PLANET 91

quite different. He wore a body suit made of some synthetic material and a light headset.

"Welcome to the Large Magellanic Cloud!" his host said. "I hope your trip was not arduous."

Setni gave a start: these words had been directed into his brain. Was this a race of telepaths?

"Not really," the Magellanite answered his mental question. "The headpiece I wear transmits your thoughts through a relay to a computer. Nothing magic in that. But I have not introduced myself. My name is Curx Verth and I am one of the Directors of Hagen. My companions are also Directors."

The astronaut had caught on: he was on the Large Magellanic Cloud. No Polluxian spacecraft had ever left the Milky Way! Those Magellanites certainly had attained a high degree of technological achievement. He could only hope that their intentions toward him were peaceful.

"Setni, Polluxian astronaut. How do you do," he stammered.

"A Polluxian?" the woman said with a frown. "There are no such people in this galaxy. Do you come from our nearest neighbor?"

"Well, yes. You ought to realize it, since you dragged me here!"

"Olxa is speaking the truth, my friend," the first man went on. "One of our machines, an advanced model of transmitter, brought you here; but we do not know about where you came from. To be perfectly frank, we find it hard to believe. How could our transmitter have been at such a distance from

Magellan? None of our expeditions has ever reached so far."

"But it's true!" the Polluxian insisted. "I don't understand it myself. I was on a planet in the Milky Way. There, I discovered hidden in a hypogeum, machines quite unfamiliar to me. I sat down in a sort of chair and here I am."

"Curious," the third person said. "He is telling the truth and yet his tale is incredible!"

"You're right, Alvador," Curx said. "All this is so baffling. Who knows? Perhaps the Rorx have set a new trap for us?"

"In any event," the young woman interrupted, "it seems very rude to pursue our investigation here. Until further notice, Setni is our guest and must be treated as such."

"How right you are, Olxa! Our friend from the Milky Way must find us discourteous. Come, we are going to take you to a more comfortable place."

Curx led the way and the foursome entered the tower. They went down several stories using an anti-G well, then they entered a room of harmonious proportions, furnished with seats placed around low tables. Setni admired the luminous frescoes on the walls, pictures that depicted unknown landscapes in iridescent colors. He sat down on a comfortable sofa.

With a gesture, Olxa summoned an assortment of drinks and snacks and invited him to help himself. The astronaut hesitated imperceptibly; all navigation codes stipulate that one must not eat or drink unknown products without analyzing them.

THE ENCHANTED PLANET 93

"Don't be afraid, dear friend. Guests are sacred to us. None of this could harm you."

Once again the answer had come before the question had been formulated; these telepaths could read his thoughts as long as he did not put up any opposition. They appeared friendly and the girl was very beautiful, so why worry? Setni, totally relaxed, settled back and poured himself a drink. Afterward, a gentle warmth filled him with a feeling of euphoria.

"All right, friends! Ask questions, but I'm afraid you will be disappointed. I don't understand what's been happening to me."

"Let's start your story at its beginning," said Alvador. "You said that you were on a planet in your Galaxy and discovered a hypogeum which contained one of our matter transmitters. What were you doing there? Did you have documentation on that star?"

"No. That's why I was sent on a reconnaissance trip, to find out where it came from and why it had appeared."

"You were right, Curx," Olxa said. "The Rorx must have transferred one of our planets to the Milky Way, but why?"

"From our friend's account, this voyage took place both in space and time, and that he comes from the distant future," Alvador observed. "But we interrupted you, Setni."

"Well, the star I was exploring was strange. Its civilization was medieval and its inhabitants looked very much like you do. One of the knights could have been your brother, Curx. No machines functioned there. Two magicians seemed to derive malicious pleasure from playing tricks on the unfortunate natives. I was obliged to fight them with my mental powers alone, as none of my gadgets worked."

"What you say is most informative," said Olxa thoughtfully. "We are fighting against monstrous entities who have chased us off one planet after another. One of their chief weapons is able to prevent us from using our missiles or our atomic gear; those fiends make them inoperative."

Setni commented, "My foes had similar powers. But tell me, where did they come from?"

"They showed up from peripheral sectors of our Galaxy, then gradually pushed us back toward the center of Magellan. I confess that we had given up thoughts of defeating them," Curx said. "However, your arrival gives us renewed hopes: you seem endowed with remarkable telepathy; you can transmit and receive messages without using equipment. Perhaps you can show us how to fight the Rorx."

Setni carefully did not reveal to his new friends the Psyborgs' cabochon, without which he would have no *psy* powers at all. He very much wanted to help the Magellanites whose fight for survival seemed to be connected with the battle he had waged on the other planet. He asked, "As I understand it, you have squadrons of spacecraft. How can you maneuver them if the Rorx render your machines inoperable?"

"You've understood the problem," Alvador answered. "We have developed systems of command operated by telepathy. Our ships obey orders transmitted mentally, we have won defensive victories. But our enemies' powerful wave lengths are now blocking our transmitters, so we have suffered major setbacks."

The Polluxian meditated before answering. Duessa and Archimago must belong to the unknown enemies of these Magellanites. He knew he outclassed them in the use of telekinesis and telepathy. Perhaps he could be of real help to Olxa and her likeable compatriots. "I think that my recent adversaries are also Rorx. They made a mysterious raid into our Milky Way. I learned to deal with their magic and defeated them. If I could make psychic contact with the Rorx, I could probably help you."

"Thanks for your assistance, noble Polluxian!" Curx exclaimed. "Unfortunately we cannot hope for miracles. Actually, my compatriots are cornered; those cursed Rorx take over our constellations unimpeded. However, if there is anything we can do for you, we'll try our best."

"Well, I don't understand how I got so far away from home in space and time. I want to know if you are in a position to help me return when I'm through with those Rorx," Setni said.

"Unfortunately I don't know. Your arrival was a great surprise. True, we are working on a time machine, which would permit a few representatives of our race to escape when the Rorx reach Hagen, our capital. Unfortunately, it is far from finished. Even if we do succeed in finishing it before our enemies come, there is the problem of its size."

"Have those fiends discovered its existence?"

"Certainly not. It is kept hidden under cliffs of impenetrable rock. But in order to function, its batteries have to store an enormous amount of energy. At the present moment, we are far from . . ."

"Yet it manifestly functions since I am here!" Setni answered.

"Yes. That's what's puzzling us. It was obviously finished before our people were destroyed; it must have stored up the necessary energy for the future."

"I see no other explanation, but that does not reassure my eventual return."

"Still, one hypothesis might explain the mystery," Olxa interrupted. "The time transmitter was designed to function automatically, when a human takes his place on the seat. It must be programmed to transport its passenger to this planet in the Large Magellanic Clouds. That's why you came here. You have some chance of getting back home for, unless reprogrammed, the machine reverses itself at the end of a month. You should be returned to your starting point."

"That's great," sighed Setni. "I hope it had enough energy stored up; but, can you use it to save yourselves?"

"I don't believe so," the young woman said sadly. "We'll never accumulate enough energy in a month. You are our only hope, if you could provide us with a way of repelling the Rorx before you return."

"I see that every minute counts. What do you suggest?"

"We are going to send out a squadron to fight our enemies and you will be on board a vessel," Curx said. "I'll assume command. During the battle, you can observe and gather information about the Rorx. Our ship will leave before the end of the battle, so you can come back to advise our scientists. OK?"

"Of course. But you will suffer tremendous losses without my being able to guarantee you results."

"We are not afraid of death: better die in battle than be trapped on this planet. Anyway, we always manage to destroy a few of their ships, so our sacrifices are not in vain."

"Good. When do we leave?"

"We'll take off at once if you're not suffering from space fatigue. Every second counts."

"OK. I'll probably have a chance to rest during the crossing."

And so Setni rode aboard the flagship of a squadron of a hundred ships, sailing across the Large Magellanic Cloud. This brought back familiar memories; he felt much more at ease than on the planet of Archimago and Duessa. When Curx and Olxa took him to central command, he was astonished by the bareness of the walls; there were no dials, no switches, no traces of any instruments.

Curx, noting his surprise, said with a smile:

"You seem puzzled.... Our spacecraft can't look very different from yours."

"Not on the outside. But I can't see how you maneuver them."

"Look," the Magellanite said, as he slid open a panel.

A soundproof room was revealed. There were five men seated in a circle, wearing headpieces connected to a machine similar to one that Setni had used during his journey through time.

"I don't understand," Setni admitted. "Are they connected to a computer?"

"You know that the enemy can block our electronic devices. So we give orders to our ships by telepathy. The astronauts see images of outer space; they give mental orders for all maneuvers and fire our defensive or offensive weapons. Would you like to see it?"

Setni was about to accept when an astronaut ran into the control room shouting: "What idiot opened the door to our circle of thought?"

"Let me introduce the ship's commandant, Stadyr. He is able, but hard to get along with."

"Delighted," stammered Setni.

"Who the hell is this outsider?" roared the astronaut. "No one is allowed into this room during operations. Circles of thought must work in absolute quiet; you know that, Curx!"

"Come on relax! Setni is our ally. He possesses remarkable psychic powers which could be of great help to us. That's why I was showing him the room."

THE ENCHANTED PLANET

"Now listen to me, Curx. You're one of the Directors, you can give me orders when we are ashore. Here, I am in sole command. Maybe he can liquidate the Rorx by himself; I couldn't care less. Right now, we are outside the zone of operations; he can play around all he likes. But I warn you, when we are in the combat zone, I don't want him underfoot."

"Don't pay any attention to him," Olxa laughed. "But the delicate balance among the astronauts in the circle of thought which pilots the ship must not be upset. We relieve them every hour, except during combat. Come on, we'll show you the auxiliary room."

Setni followed his two friends to the other room. He thought the Magellanites treated their superiors casually; no astronaut in the Confederation would dare speak to a member of the Great Council that way.

Curx placed headphones on him. The astronaut was startled to see the surrounding constellations in such extraordinary relief that he was able to precisely gauge their distance. He could literally feel the forward progress of the spaceship and could speed it up or slow it down. He had become the brain of a ship, whose pulsations he could feel.

He lost his bearings for a while, his orders producing sudden jerky maneuvers. But he very quickly learned to regulate his movements and the turns became smoother. When Curx removed the thin helmet, he felt he had become quite familiar with this new method.

"This was only a mock-up, naturally," Olxa informed him. "You were not actually directing the spaceship, but I must say you are skillful."

"You're astonishing," Curx chimed in. "Your psychic powers are much better than ours. It takes five Magellanites to do what you did alone! Each one is in charge of a particular function: search, maneuvers, weaponry, ship-to-ship coordination, monitoring of ship's functions. You are able to do it all. Are your compatriots as able as you?"

"Well," the astronaut said evasively, "I'm pretty well known in the Polluxian fleet. However, I'm not the best."

"Well, if we had such psychic powers we'd have much less trouble with those damned Rorx! Could you start training regularly?"

"Oh, I feel in great shape," Setni assured them.

"In that case, I'll speak to Stadyr: he'll have to submit. I want you at the controls when we make contact with the Rorx. Our circles of thought concentrate great amounts of energy on enemy ships; one time in ten this disintergrates them. You must make trial runs with remote control guidance and I am sure you'll get results."

"OK. I hope you won't be disappointed."

The following day, Setni went into training; the speed with which he mastered the new techniques filled his friends with admiration. Actually this was easy for Setni; his cabochon enormously amplified his feeble *psy* capabilities. Obviously it remained to be seen whether this would work against the Rorx.

The astronaut also had time to find out how

THE ENCHANTED PLANET

Magellanites lived. They were governed by the Board of Three: Curx, Olxa and Alvador. It was surprising that two of them were willing to go into battle, but it showed the liberal character of their civilization. Relations between individuals were quite easy; everyone had a voice, which explained Stadyr's attitude. Each citizen was free and not just a number lost among masses. Every Magellanite participated in government by voting for triumvirate every year. Unless the directors made a major blunder, they often remained in power for years. A request by fifty percent of the electorate was enough to call for a new election. Relations among citizens were also uncomplicated, perhaps because they knew the end might be near. They realized they wanted to make the best of the brief time remaining.

However, Setni was considerably surprised when, one evening, the charming Olxa made it clear she would like to make love with him. It must be admitted that Magellanites were hedonists and libertines who indulged in frequent binges. The beautiful lady was often somewhat tipsy.

Setni, flabbergasted, looked about him at a party that was turning into an orgy; the men openly made passes at the women.

"Don't you want me?" Olxa coaxed.

"Sure, but . . ."

"You don't think I'm pretty?"

"You're very beautiful!"

"Then why resist? Are you impotent?" she asked, frowning.

"Certainly not! Don't you see, we belong to different worlds..."

"What difference does that make?" she said, becoming insistent.

"Oh, Olxa. Not in front of all these people!"

"Polluxians are shy. OK, come to my stateroom."

"It's not a question of caution!" Setni answered.

"What then?"

"Well, I love another woman: a marvelous creature. I want to be faithful to her."

"She'll never know."

"I disagree. If I were to be unfaithful, I could never again look her in the eye," Setni declared emotionally.

"What an idiot you are! In a few months I'll be dead; you too, if the transferer doesn't work. So we should enjoy life while we can."

"Believe me, I think you're beautiful, Olxa, but Nicolette is even more beautiful. If I die, it will be with a picture of her before my eyes."

"You're hopeless," Olxa grumbled. "I have lots of other admirers, only I did want to know how Galaxites perform."

Thereupon she turned away from Setni and was soon in the arms of another man who responded to her advances. The astronaut looked around him: suddenly exhausted, he left and took refuge in his stateroom.

He could understand those people. An approaching cataclysm tends to unleash reactions of this sort. People condemned to death want to enjoy the last moments of life. Actually, it was remarkable that the Magellanite civilization had not sunk into chaos. Their astronauts had not given up hope of victory, which explained the continuation of a certain discipline.

Commandant Stadyr, however, was reacting differently. The desperate position the Magellanite forces had, if anything, made him more intractable; it reinforced his religious fanaticism. He categorically refused to entrust his ship to an outsider, so that Curx had to train his candidate secretly. When zero hour came, there was bound to be a clash.

The squadron continued its journey into space. Quite soon, the circles of thought picked up the first enemy formations. Setni was able to study them, along with the other astronauts aboard, on screens permanently focused on space. A few surveyor vessels joined the fleet. Their assignment was to stay in touch, without taking part in the battle. A rosy nebula glimmered in the distance. In its neighborhood were several rich planets still inhabited by Magellanites.

Curx found Setni in his stateroom and discreetly gave him his final instructions. "First, I shall maneuver the circle of thought to which Stadyr belongs. Probably the results will be disappointing and our ships will be destroyed, one after the other. You will then take over. I hope you'll be more effective."

"Fine. I'll try not to let you down."

"You're our last chance. Come," Curx murmured. They both went to the control room where

Setni had spent many hours. He sat down, carefully adjusting his headpiece.

At first, he received messages from the planets in the local system. Their inhabitants entertained no false hopes; they thanked their compatriots for attempting to fight the enemy, then assured them they were prepared to die with dignity. Soon, the Magellanite spaceships made contact with the invading fleet. In the ensuing battle, which took place in the rosy nebula, the Rorx easily gained the upper hand. Snakes of fire materialized near the Magellanite ships which, once they had been touched, drifted away lifeless without any visible damage.

This war was quite unlike anything that took place and the planet of the Knight of the Purple Cross. Setni did not at first understand the technique of the aggressors. One after the other, their own ships were put out of commission; occasionally a Rorx unit suffered, but the ratio of losses was ten to one, just as Curx predicted.

Then, the fiery snakes came close to the flagship. "Get in there now, Setni!" shouted Curx, throwing the switch.

The astronaut was prepared, but not for the strong psychic shock he received. He felt as though his brain would burst and that his limbs were paralyzed. But reacting quickly, Setni launched a psychic counter-attack and found that the frightening sensation had vanished. In a frenzy of hatred, he focused destructive thoughts on an enemy ship, as he had done to Duessa's and Archimago's castle.

He was delighted to see his target disintegrate, leaving no trace.

He barely heard Curx's cry of joy; he was concentrating on another objective which also disappeared. But it was too late: the enemy's numerical superiority was too great. The Rorx were closing in on the flagship in a pincer movement. Setni had to greatly increase the ship's power to make a retreat. He destroyed six more enemy ships before moving out of range.

Fortunately, the Magellanite flagship was one of the fastest in the fleet, so it managed to shed its pursuers. But before the rosy nebula vanished from sight, the Magellanites witnessed the landing of the Rorx on planets left to their sad fate. The invaders resembled crabs. Hordes of them descended upon the cities, massacring everyone, laying waste everything in sight.

Setni was horrified. Was this fate in store for his own compatriots? Were Archimago and Duessa scouts sent to test the resistance of the people of the Milky Way? In that case, he had better return home quickly.

Chapter VII

Setni removed his headset: he felt as though his head would burst. It had been a hard fight, harder than his previous ones against Duessa and Archimago. This was not surprising since he had just repelled the *psy* powers of countless Rorx.

He was too absorbed in his analysis of the battle to reply to Curx's paeons of praise. The latter was exultant: Setni's psychic power was much greater than he had thought; if he could discover how Setni had pushed back the countless enemy forces, his country might be saved. Setni was recovering from his exhaustion and soon answered the Magellanite's questions.

"Do all your compatriots possess such powers?"

"Unfortunately no," grumbled the astronaut. "In fact, most of them are even less skilled than yours."

"How do you account for your *psy* powers?"

"I underwent special training," Setni replied evasively.

"Yet, the configuration of your brain does not seem especially adapted to transmit. Do you have a special amplifier? Please be honest with me! You could avert frightful genocide! Our fate is in your hands."

The astronaut hesitated to divulge the secret of the cabochon. If these people learned of it, they would ask to examine it. If they were to wreck it, he'd lose all his powers. What would happen to the Polluxians if, upon his return, Archimago and Duessa learned of his weakness? There would be an invasion, and the Milky Way would suffer the same fate as the Large Magellanic Cloud. Curx seemed to guess what was holding him back.

"I can assure you that if there is an amplifier, our scientists will examine it with utmost care. I also guarantee it will not be damaged," Curx promised.

"Yes, I do have an amplifier; a gadget hidden inside this cabochon. I myself don't know how it works."

"I do thank you! Will you let our specialists examine it when we get back to Hagen?"

"Yes, I promise," Setni said.

Curx accompanied his guest to his stateroom where he fell into a deep sleep. He remained perfectly still for hours, completely prostrated. Curx and Olxa took turns keeping an eye on him. Setni finally came to and restored his strength with a hearty meal and drink.

A few hours later, when he was feeling refreshed, Stadyr burst into the stateroom.

"Look," he said, "you've got something coming to you. Your goddamned interference has cost me the loss of my command. I'm the laughing stock of the whole crew. You'll have to make it up to me."

Curx tried to intervene. "Come on, Stadyr. Don't be angry! Our friend had nothing to do with that. The responsibility rests entirely with me; I am the one who pulled the switch."

"You're not going to tell me that this alien was not at the controls of *my* ship at the crucial moment."

"True. But you have not been relieved of your command. He was acting under my orders."

"That doesn't change a thing. I have been dishonored and I have the right to fight a duel with him."

"Come on, Stadyr," Olxa intervened. "Be reasonable: if he had not wiped out some of our enemies, we wouldn't be here having this discussion."

"But that man took my place and made me look incompetent: he'll have to take the consequences. Our laws are explicit in this matter."

Curx and Olxa seemed perplexed. They quietly exchanged a few words. Then the young woman said: "All right. We cannot deny your rights. But you cannot fight until we're back in Hagen. Duels are forbidden on warships."

"OK. I won't disobey, but I want to make sure I meet him after we have landed. We'll discuss weapons later." The officer saluted and left.

"What an idiotic to-do," grumbled Setni. "There is no reason for me to meet that imbecile. As if I didn't have enough problems!"

"But our laws are very strict; you owe him reparation," said Curx.

"Suppose the Board were to postpone the duel?" suggested Olxa.

"On what grounds?"

"Because Setni is indispensable to help us make amplifiers like his."

"But he has admitted that he knows nothing about it."

"What difference does that make? No one else need know."

"How clever women are," Curx said, with a smile. "Of course, all we need do is wait until the transmitter carries our friend back to his own time period in the Milky Way!"

"Providing it functions," Setni thought. He wondered it he'd ever get home again.

Olxa's ruse worked remarkably well. The Board, apprised of the problem, agreed whole-heartedly. Setni regretfully parted with his cabochon and the scientists of Hagen examined it under his supervision.

The Magellanites were remarkable technicians, ahead of Setni's compatriots in many ways. They had no difficulty in extracting the case from the precious stone. But when they saw the extraordinary microminiaturized mechanism inside, they admitted defeat: not one of them could duplicate this gem of technology.

But they did not give up. They made X-rays and tomographs in successive stages, which showed the structure of the delicate machine. The technicians worked all day long, in shifts. But they made no real progress.

Setni finally got tired of watching them work and explored the city in the company of Olxa, who seemed more in love than ever, despite his efforts to discourage her. They visited a number of museums where Setni was able to admire some remarkable art by Magellanites. Fluorescent paintings with mobile motifs drew his attention. But what he liked best were the technical exhibits showing the story of various disciplines and scientific achievements.

Then, he had a stroke of genius: he was examining an armor-plated satellite whose function was to measure the radiation of stars. "I wonder why my cabochon functioned in the face of Rorx attacks? Didn't you tell me they emitted fields of interference which affected all instruments built on the principles of physics?"

"You're right. We must tell our research teams. The cabochon must have some sort of protective shield. If we could find out what it is, we'd almost be there!" Olxa cried out.

The Magellanite scientists soon found a solution; a thin layer of selenium rendered a mechanism impervious to the Rorx field. Obviously, they could not protect all spaceships with a layer of that metal. Setni suggested that perhaps they could build missiles with anti-matter warheads, equipped with automatic detonators that were plated with selenium.

The specialists instantly approved and experimented along those lines. They were successful. Setni's reputation with the Magellanites skyrocketed. The technicians kept asking for advice, which

THE ENCHANTED PLANET

he found embarrassing as he was less knowledgeable than they.

Bombs of this type were quickly put into production and Setni promised he would accompany the squadron which made the first real tests on enemy ships. All this took time, which enabled him to continue his sight-seeing in the city.

The research, naturally, was top secret. No one on the outside knew there was a faint hope of defeating the Rorx. Therefore the people of Hagen continued to behave as if their extinction was inevitable.

The wise calmly went about their business, seeking solace in religion and carrying out their civic or family duties. Others plunged into debauchery, trying to fit into a few months the pleasures of a lifetime. However, extremist groups were disturbing the peace. They claimed that the cataclysm threatening them was just retribution for their sins, that it was impious to resist it.

Commandant Stadyr had been won over by these fanatics. Furious at Setni's escape, with the connivance of the Board, he thirsted for revenge. He easily convinced the Believers in the Last Days that this alien constituted a real danger to their religious sect. Wasn't he working on a weapon to fight the Rorx; this would result in increasing their hatred for the Magellanites.

The commandant persuaded them that if they captured the stranger, the research could not continue. So, with their support, Stadyr began to track his foe. He noticed that Setni went out every morning to see the sights. Olxa, whenever she was free, would accompany him. Most of the museums were empty, the citizens of Hagen having other things to worry about. The guards also relaxed their surveillance, frequently leaving their posts.

Stadyr chose his time carefully. With the help of some strong-armed fanatics, he began to stalk his prey. He did not have to wait long. One day, Setni was in an empty museum looking at a vast diorama showing biological evolution on Magellan. Five thugs jumped him from their hiding place, in a huge reproduction of a saurian.

Setni, without his cabochon, was unable to use his *psy* powers. A sack was thrown over his head, then his oppressors pushed him down and trussed him up. His assailants threw him into a packing case. They donned clothes stolen from the cloakroom and, thus disguised, calmly left the museum without attracting any attention.

The packing case was placed in a van parked in front of the museum, which then went to the suburbs. Stadyr made sure that they were not followed. No one had witnessed the kidnapping and the thugs reached their hiding-place undisturbed. There was an underground network beneath the city. Some rooms were visited regularly, but most tunnels had been abandoned. Magellanites were not familiar with their interminable windings.

The unfortunate Setni found himself in a dark cell with rusty but solid grates. He didn't know where he was, nor who his captors were. He had been trapped, with little hope of being freed. The

THE ENCHANTED PLANET

transmitter could probably not bring the voyager back to his own time period; his prison was located under a thick layer of rocks. He bitterly regretted having lent the Psyborgs' cabochon, his best safeguard in a hostile world. Here he was, a prisoner, with little or no hope of regaining his freedom.

He couldn't keep track of time. Every so often a grating was opened and a hand pushed a bowl of slop through it. Setni would place a stone on a small heap, not knowing whether the periods between meals constituted a day in local time. It probably bore no relation to time on Archimago's planet.

Despite the loss of the cabochon, Setni had retained some of his former mental powers. He could actually "feel" the presence of other captives near his cell, without being able to transmit any message to them.

The prisoner spent most of his time fighting off rat-like animals who tried to bite him several times. A plank from his bed served as his weapon. Fortunately, he could hear them moving in the silence. His aggressors learned to treat him with respect and stopped trying to eat him up alive.

At last, just as he had almost lost all hope, he heard footsteps in the corridor. The door opened wide. Setni, blinded by the torchlight, shaded his eyes. A rough hand grabbed him by the collar of his tunic. A voice growled: "Come on and don't be smart."

Setni had difficulty understanding the local language: again he keenly felt the loss of his cabochon. So with the two guards, he walked through the vaulted tunnel. One lout amused himself by poking Setni in the ribs with his sword.

The prisoner's eyes gradually became used to the light and he was able to make out the clothes of the man in front of him. Curiously enough, he was dressed in medieval armor, similar to that worn by the people of Archimago's planet. Had he again been shifted in time?

A hundred yards or so further, they emerged into a large hall lit by torches set in walls sweating with dampness. This was apparently some sort of tribunal, for three judges sat on a dais. Setni saw instruments of torture. The executioner, who was dead drunk, was sprawled out alongside a wooden bench.

The guards roughly pushed Setni forward. He was convinced he had only a few moments to live.

"So this is the foreigner we have heard so much about. Your name?"

"Setni."

"Nationality?"

"Polluxian. I lived in a distant Galaxy."

"I find that hard to believe. You don't speak our language very well," the judge growled.

"We've been over all that," another magistrate interrupted. "The Board is aware of it."

"Really? That's odd. But it does not alter the case!"

"Perhaps our brave Rorx ally would like to speak about this?" suggested the third judge, looking at a hooded figure hunched up in a dark corner.

THE ENCHANTED PLANET 115

Setni heard nothing, but the panel of judges seemed to have been given their answer because the chairman went on:

"Very well. In that case we'll proceed to the charges brought against him."

So, Setni thought, these Rorx fiends have already managed to infiltrate Hagen without the knowledge of the Board. The situation is even worse than Curx realizes.

The voice droned on. "This foreigner deliberately opposed the Rorx and, according to our information, was helping to manufacture new weapons. He must be deactivated. Indeed, to bring peace to the Large Cloud the fight against the Rorx must be stopped. With their mercy, they are willing to save the lives of some of us who will return to an ancestral way of life; and we must give up all psychic and scientific research."

The sinister hooded shape stirred and seemed to be giving an order to the judge, for he stopped to say: "As you wish, noble Rorx! Please enlighten us as to the exact misdeeds of this reprehensible foreigner."

Setni was horrified to feel a thought inserted into his brain, searching his memory to find out what had been achieved in the laboratories of Hagen. With some bitterness, he congratulated himself on having perfected a worthwhile technique, since the enemy was taking the trouble to search his mind. Then he tried to fight off the Rorx, in vain. Without the cabochon, he was as helpless as a child.

Just then, a portion of the ceiling fell. Plaster

and stones wounded some of the guards. A dozen men dropped to the ground, pistols in hand. Spurts of flame mowed down the remaining soldiers. The flames flickered and went out: the Rorx were now counter-attacking. Tongues of fire began to weave, snake-like, in the air, striking down some of the rescuers.

Setni stood riveted, unable to act. Just then, Curx leapt to his side and plunged a knife into a guard who tried to interfere. He encircled Setni's waist with the belt carrying the cabochon.

Setni regained his powers instantly. He repelled the little flames threatening him and concentrated on fighting the Rorx. The hodded creature quickly felt the psychic powers of his foe and tried to ward off the attack. Meanwhile Curx's companions were putting the members of the tribunal and soldiers out of commission.

Setni was furiously trying to disintegrate his adversary. The latter was no stronger than Archimago and Duessa: the cabochon gradually caused the hooded figure to fade; he became diaphanous, translucent, then disappeared altogether. Setni didn't know whether it was a psychic materialization or a real Rorx, but his opponent was no longer there.

"Well, it looks as if I'd arrived just in time!" Curx exclaimed.

"You did! A few moments more and I'd have been strangled. But tell me, how did you find me?"

"With the help of that marvelous gadget I've just returned to you. It had preserved the imprint of your thoughts; one of the scientists finally noticed it. We searched Hagen and at last we felt a faint tremor. Of course, we had a hard time locating you in this maze. Luckily I was able to find a copy of the tunnel's plan in our archives, that saved a little time."

"Incidentally, how long was I a prisoner?"

"Eight days, by our reckoning."

"Is that all? I thought I'd been here for at least a month," Setni sighed.

"I can see why. Incidentally, who was that creature in the corner?"

"A Rorx."

"What! Those fiends have already infiltrated Hagen?"

"I'm not absolutely sure. It may have been a psychic phenomenon. But to be sure, you'd better have these tunnels thoroughly searched."

"Don't worry: we'll set up a guard. Unfortunately, there are so many hidden places that I'm afraid we shan't catch them. The important thing is that you're safe. Let's go back outside."

They talked as they went and Setni learned that the Hagen technicians had produced some weapons built according to his specifications. The anti-matter warheads were protected by a layer of selenium and the detonator was set off by psychic means. Curx asked him if he would accompany a fighting squadron equipped with the new missiles, to make sure they functioned properly.

Setni was glad to take part in the expedition: if the experiment worked, the Magellanites would have an effective weapon they could mass-produce.

This would give them an appreciable advantage in fighting the Rorx.

The scientists had also begun to understand how the cabochon worked. Its source of energy was the lines of the planets' magnetic fields; or, at times, the Galaxy's. This explained its huge energy potential. On the other hand, the microminiaturization of the gadget posed problems. The technicians could produce a replica of the amplifier on a larger scale, but to finish it would take a year. Would it be possible to keep the Rorx at bay until then? Curx did not think so.

Nonetheless, this research was not useless; they could perfect the transmitter which the Magellanites had built in a deep, secret crypt.

Setni came out into the open air with great pleasure. Olxa greeted him joyously and tried to make him forget the wretched hours spent in the catacombs of Hagen. However, his hosts wanted him to appear as a witness against the men who had kidnapped him. Curx was counting heavily on his telepathic abilities to find out the whole truth.

The Polluxian took little pleasure in confronting his former tormentors before a tribunal in Hagen. Stadyr sat among the defendants.

Alvador, who represented the Board, questioned him first. "How could an astronaut, with a remarkable record like yours, become an accomplice of our greatest enemies?" he wondered.

The commandant replied unhesitatingly: "Simple opportunism! Because of my position, I know we have no hope of winning this war. I believe that it is essential that some Magellanites survive. We must make a deal with the Rorx and since you refused to, I became a Believer in the Last Days."

"What is the goal of this subversive group?"

"To make contact with the Rorx in order to bargain. We have been assured that members of the BLD will be spared. The Rorx are willing to allow some Magellanites to remain on their planets, providing they cease making scientific experiments."

"Are you saying that a few of our compatriots still live on some of the occupied planets?"

"I know they do, I've seen them! Obviously their life, in a medieval style, is entirely different from ours. But that doesn't keep them from being happy. On the contrary! Our technological civilization brings only rot and degradation to humans."

Setni signalled to Alvador; he wanted to ask a few questions, so the director gave him the floor.

"Tell me, Stadyr, do they appear to be content?"

"I can't really tell. All I've seen are Rorx psychic projections."

"Well, I can tell you what happens to your compatriots when the Rorx take over. Magellanites are taken from their parents when they are infants and are conditioned not to rebel. I have seen a planet which these vile creatures rule: they enjoy torturing their subjects and see them suffer. They create monstrous entities who chase their denfenseless victims. Do you still think it would be better to stop fighting?"

The astronaut did not reply. He frowned, in deep

thought. Then he grumbled: "Why struggle hopelessly if we'll be defeated? I have seen my best friends, the bravest, die in space by the score."

"You are forgetting our Polluxian friend," Alvador said. "Thanks to him, we now have new weapons which soon will be tested. Your defeatism is inexcusable, especially after you made it possible for the Rorx to spy on us in Hagen. Are there many of them on our planet?"

"Actually, I've seen only one: the one Setni killed. How did he do it? No one else was ever able to touch him."

"Wasn't he simply an image projected by some machine brought into the catacombs?"

"That's possible," admitted the astronaut. "The Prophet of the Believers has a chapel, which only the Initiate are allowed to enter. I have told you everything I know: I happened to brush against the master and I felt nothing there."

"Could you give us more particulars about that Prophet?"

"No. I've told too much already. You'll never defeat the Rorx: you'll all die a horrible death. Stop the fighting, while there is still time; perhaps you will be spared."

In spite of Alvador's efforts, Stadyr refused to answer any more questions. The director then signalled to Setni to probe the defendant's brain.

Setni did so easily, but discovered nothing new. An efficient system of compartmentation protected the Believers of the Last Days. The Commandant really knew nothing further and he was sincere in advising the Magellanites to ask for an armistice.

While Alvador went on questioning the other defendants, Setni withdrew, pensively. It appeared, clearly, that the Rorx would rule the Magellanites. Archimago's planet was a replica of the one Stadyr described. Ought he not advise Curx to give up his futile efforts, which only further antagonized the Rorx?

Chapter VIII

The trial was quickly over. The judges decided to be severe in order to stimulate the Magellanites' fighting spirit. Stadyr and the Believers of the Last Days were condemned to death. According to custom, traitors to the nation were put to death in the public square. This was a gruesome execution.

The prisoners were put inside the skins of maours, a kind of marine mammal. Only their heads protruded. As the skins dried out, they shrank. The executioner began by sprinkling them with water and gradually the skins shrivelled up, grinding up the victims who screamed in agony.

Setni did not witness this torture. He disapproved of capital punishment, especially under these circumstances. He spent most of his time with the scientists, who were putting the finishing touches on the anti-matter warhead missiles. Their production was under way and in a few days, the squadron could leave on its test mission.

Also, Curx gave him another assignment: at this time of year, the continent on which Hagen was located suffered devastating tropical hurricanes.

THE ENCHANTED PLANET

Satellites could forecast their arrival, but could not stop the damage they wrought.

He learned from a bulletin issued by the weather bureau that a small coastal city had, strangely, been spared by the cyclone. Curx was still trying to find where the Believers of the Last Days had concealed the transmitter with which the Rorx projected their effigies on the planet. The meteorological phenomenon seemed odd, so he told Setni of his suspicions and asked him to investigate.

Setni gladly accepted; he probably couldn't change the fate of the Magellanites, but he wanted to try to help them in any way. He took a glider and, with Olxa, flew over the little town.

Everything appeared normal, people calmly went about their business, fishing boats sailed out of the harbor; there was no trace of spaceships or of any sort of installation. But through his cabochon, Setni could clearly feel hostile forces present. He mentioned this to Olxa.

"You're sure it's Rorx?" she asked.

"Absolutely. I can always recognize it now. They are sticky and false; none of your compatriots has a psychism like it."

"That's incredible. How do they manage to penetrate to the core of our defenses? The future looks grim for us."

Setni refrained from telling her he felt even more pessimistic than she. There was absolutely nothing to stop the Magellanites from being enslaved by the Rorx.

"What do you expect? Their psychic powers are

so great that they can easily hoodwink your compatriots. I don't believe there are many of them here, but they are trying to learn about me. My arrival was a great surprise to them."

"Can you spot them?"

"I think they are hiding along this rocky coast, probably inside some hidden grotto. The BLD probably reach it by boat."

"What are we going to do? I can give an order to have it bombarded by one of our missiles. Unfortunately, I'm afraid such an explosion would kill a great many of our people. And if we evacuate them, the Rorx would suspect they had been spotted."

"I'll deal with them alone, I'm not afraid. With my amplifier..."

"As you like, but be careful. Remember: you're now our only hope."

The glider landed on a small sandy beach, not far from a cliff. Olxa took off at once, and Setni was alone.

He walked along the shore, picking up shells like an ordinary hiker. The sound of the surf, the briny smell of seaweed, reminded him of his native planet; he began to daydream about this world that was so distant and yet so like his.

Soon, his mind became clearer; he had located the invaders' hiding place, a dark grotto, at sea level. Setni entered the dark cavern without a qualm. His foes must have spotted him so he concentrated all his psychic powers on repelling their attack.

THE ENCHANTED PLANET

It was not long in coming; they conjured up a hideous serpent which dashed forward on its short legs and lunged at the intruder. Its gaping jaw revealed rows of deadly fangs. It would put to flight any Magellanite; the monster's scaly exterior was weapon proof. But Setni didn't use normal weapons. Stretching out his arm, he aimed a blinding fire at the monster, singeing his sides, making him retreat, with howls of pain, into the depths of the cavern where he disappeared.

The Rorx, bowing to superior power, changed tactics at once. As soon as the astronaut had entered the cavern, luminescent spots began to whirl in front of his eyes. Their hypnotic power made Setni call upon all his strength to repel the suggestions they conjured up. Never before had he been subjected to such assault, even when combatting Archimago and Duessa. The black rocks had vanished, and a green plain stretched before him, like the one on the planet of the Knight of the Purple Cross. Rorx technique seemed not to change.

Suddenly, shrubbery appeared. Birds sang in its bright foliage. Angelic voices mingled with their song. Then, the astronaut saw a seductive beauty languidly lying on a bed of roses. She was clad in a diaphanous silvery veil through which could be seen her milk-white skin. Her snowy breasts beckoned invitingly, an enticing smile allowed a glimpse of pearly teeth.

In spite of himself, Setni began to think of the marvelous women from Sirius, the greatest beauties of the Milky Way; this nymph made a mock of their beauty. Her aquamarine eyes, her moist lips beckoned irresistibly. Setni took a step forward, everything else in the universe had become unimportant.

But from deep inside him, a small image emerged: Nicolette, with arms outstretched, had come between him and the lascivious enchantress. He regained his self-control at once. Enraged by the trick, he unleashed his bolts of lightning on the shrubbery and the Elf it contained. A stench of burning flesh filled his nostrils; he neutralized it with the delicate scent of carnations. Then, like a hero unbound, he sprang to attack the monstrous entities hiding behind the rocks.

He felt their strength waver; he saw four hooded figures cowering around a cubic block, licked by small crimson flames. Their vibrations became less perceptible. The Rorx appeared in their real form: hideous crustaceans with pedunculate eyes, limbs terminating in half open pincers, as though they were going to grab and tear him apart.

With a final superhuman effort, Setni, fighting down nausea, penetrated the tortuous minds of his foes. He finally let go, unleashing his great hatred. One after the other, the evil creatures disintegrated. All that remained was the cubic block, now completely colorless. Then, the installation went up in smoke.

The vault of the cavern crumbled under the impact of the conflagration. Setni had to marshall his remaining strength to conjure up a protective screen against the falling rocks. He escaped from this demonic lair and no Rorx would again haunt Hagen.

The glider was waiting for him on the shore and Olxa ran forward to meet him. "Any trouble?" she asked anxiously.

"This time there were four of them. They must have been using an amplifying device. I had a hard time repelling their hypnors."

"What counts is you're still alive."

"That shows we're on the right track. Perhaps they can be pushed back by your new weapons. Well, you can relax a bit: there are no more Rorx on this planet now."

With the help of the young woman, Setni boarded the glider and returned to Hagen. Olxa had told Curx and Alvador about Setni's victory. They congratulated him warmly upon his return.

"And now perhaps we could try the missiles," Curx suggested. "A squadron of our spaceships is ready."

"OK. After this defeat, the Rorx are not going to try direct attacks. I imagine they are disappointed not to have captured my cabochon. Let's take advantage of this breather to try a diversionary tactic. Are there many ships equipped with the new antimissiles?"

"There is an entire squadron in readiness, waiting for the results of our test. It will get into action as soon as I give them the green light," Curx said.

"Great. Let's hope that everything works properly. What about the time machine?"

"We're speeding up work on it; we benefit from

the things we've learned from your cabochon," Curx reassured him.

"Be careful with it!" Setni said with a laugh. "I am vitally interested."

The ships had been carefully selected for this flash raid. They were the fastest in the fleet. Setni was impressed by their performance. Their commandant, also, was considerably more accommodating than the unfortunate Stadyr.

Curx went on board with Setni. Alvador remained on Hagen with Olxa. The Magellanite left with a whole squadron, as soon as the two scouting vessels had returned and reported on their raid. The crossing was uneventful.

Setni had no difficulty in familiarizing himself with the commands of the dispatch boats, so he spent most of his time talking with Curx, in order to find out more about this likeable people. He learned that before the arrival of the Rorx, the Magellanites had always lived in peace. They had been traveling in space for about ten generations and had carved out a flourishing empire for themselves. The various colonies traded peacefully with one another. Several humanoid races had been assimilated by them, their level of civilization having been less advanced than that of Hagen. There had never been a war, and at that time the Magellanites had only a token fleet.

When several planets signalled the arrival of foreign spaceships, no one was concerned. But soon, all communication with them was cut off. The spaceships sent to reconnoiter picked up a few sig-

THE ENCHANTED PLANET

nals, learned there had been a massive attack and all the colonists had been massacred.

This peaceful people, faced with so brutal an invasion, did a 180 degree turn. They converted their industry and turned out a war fleet in record time. Men and women worked side by side, with full equality.

Unfortunately, every engagement with the enemy was a disaster. One after another, Magellan's former possessions fell into the hands of the invaders whose technology rendered human weapons inoperative. It was only the great distances to be covered which slowed the progress of the Rorx.

When Setni arrived, this struggle had been going on for two generations. The unexpected arrival of an inhabitant of the Milky Way had rekindled hope in the hearts of the Board members. Setni's recent successes had reinforced their hopes. If anti-matter missiles could keep the Rorx away from Hagen, perhaps there would be time to manufacture amplifiers similar to the one in the cabochon?

Such was the important mission of these six spaceships. This explained Curx's nervousness. He appeared preoccupied during the entire journey. One evening, the Magellanite came to see Setni in his stateroom and said to him:

"My friend, I must speak with you alone."

"What's the matter?"

"I have a confession to make. Stadyr's betrayal was a great shock. He was an extraordinarily able astronaut; he must have really believed in doing what he did."

"He simply didn't think you could win. He was trying to save his own skin by collaborating with the enemy—not unusual under the circumstances. Believe me, we've seen much worse in the Confederation!" Setni said.

"Yes, of course. But Stadyr would never have betrayed us if he had not believed in the possibility of co-existence with the Rorx. That's what I decided to find out, once and for all; by making a raid on an enemy-occupied planet, we will know how our compatriots are treated."

"No half measures with you, old man. What do the other Board members think?"

"I haven't told them."

"Why put me in the picture?" Setni was puzzled.

"Because I need you. Your psychic powers will allow us to make a secret inspection of a planet and find out what is going on."

"Well, that seems reasonable. But I don't see how we're going to cover such a distance in so short a time. We're supposed to test the missiles, then return to base."

"Don't worry, I've taken care of that. You probably know that the configuration of the universe, which is of non-Euclidean structure, allows for shortcuts. Since our departure, we have been following a break in space-time. We are soon going to be on occupied territory."

"You might have warned me!" Setni said indignantly.

"I was afraid you'd turn me down. Now you can't. We are nearing one of our former colonies.

THE ENCHANTED PLANET

Five spaceships will remain under cover while we try to land secretly and mingle with the population. Afterward, we'll meet the other ships and attack the local garrison. Their spaceships will come to the rescue and we'll soon find out if our new missiles are effective."

"You're crazy! What makes you think you can pull it off?"

"I can't bear the uncertainty. I must know what will happen to us if we lose this war," Curx said.

"OK, count me in," said Setni simply. "But on one condition. . . . Our five spaceships are bound to be detected and we'll never be able to inspect the planet without interference. Let me do it my way. I know the Rorx and I guarantee the outcome. We'll have carried out our assignment successfully and in the shortest time possible."

"OK, you take over the controls. I have complete confidence in you."

Setni settled down in front of the instrument panel, put on his headpiece and started issuing orders to the other spaceships. Curx saw to his amazement that the squadron was steadily heading for the occupied planet.

A few moments later radar signals were picked up, as the fleet had been spotted. The Magellanite cast a worried look at Setni who looked stolidly ahead.

"See here, we're going to have the whole Rorx fleet on our backs," the Director observed.

"Right. I even know that their two garrison ships have just taken off. We'll soon know whether our missiles are functioning properly. But first, I'm going to play games with them."

The squadron, at an order from Setni, made an about-face, fleeing at top speed. Its pursuers were gradually gaining on them. The Rorx ships were not yet within "psychic range", but would soon be. The spaceships were now too far from the planet to be within range of their radar. Setni registered the messages transmitted by the spherical ships and finally announced:

"Watch closely. We're going to find out whether our weapons are adequate."

A volley of missiles was released by the six spaceships from Hagen. Curx clearly heard the Rorx orders to destroy. In spite of the field of interference, the projectiles continued toward their objective.

This seemed to throw the two enemy captains into a panic. They tried to strengthen their emissions, but to no avail. Had it been a conventional battle, this would have been the moment to launch interceptors. Unfortunately for the Rorx, confident in their fields of interference, they hadn't any. So the missiles, uninterepted, homed in on them.

Curx shouted with joy. "Terrific! Perhaps we stand some chance of keeping those bastards away from our shores. But tell me something, the explosions seemed pretty feeble to me. Was that because the field of interference was only partially attenuated?"

"Not at all. I purposely limited the strength of the missiles to keep the Rorx from finding out about the destruction of their ships. Look, now."

The Director looked at the screen and saw the two spaceships, apparently moving intact.

"What's going on?" he fumed. "They haven't even been touched."

"That's what the Rorx will think, if they are still receiving their *psy* transmissions. A message is being sent that our ships are very fast and they will have to give chase before they can catch up with us. That way, no one will suspect..."

"But how can we land without being spotted? Their detective devices must still be functioning."

"Of course! But they've become too sure of themselves. They don't realize that their radar screens project only my mental images. In other words, they are going to think that our ships are retreating at top speed. Their instruments won't pick up our ship when it lands near their capital," Setni explained.

"Absolutely fantastic. What would we do without you?"

"Never mind that. We haven't much time. We'll have to be disguised, not to attract attention. I've been able to locate a few of your former compatriots, wearing outfits like those worn on the planet I have just left. Come on; the automatic pilot will land the spaceship in some peaceful corner."

Everything went off as Setni planned. Shortly thereafter Curx and Setni, in rags, were walking down a dusty road winding toward a shabby town. It was dominated by the imposing mass of a medieval castle with thick walls.

"Say, what language do they speak," Curx whispered.

"Yours."

"You don't think we're taking foolish chances? Why come here when you could probably give me a psychic picture of what is going on here? That was all I wanted."

"Good for you. I see you're not losing your critical faculties. But I do see everything that is happening here, except in one place: the dungeon of the fortress. I am very curious about that."

"I see. Since you know what's happened to my poor compatriots, could you fill me in a bit?"

"Of course. It's pretty depressing: they have been reduced to a state of slavery and put to work at the most repellent chores. In order to stop any rebellion, they must periodically report to a place called the 'ancestral tombs,' taking with them all children over the age of seven. That's all I have been able to learn, because a hypnotic barrier prevents them from finding out what happens when they get there. One thing is sure: they must undergo a psychic treatment that puts them entirely at the mercy of the Rorx."

"What for?"

"I don't know. Personally, I think those Rorx enjoy human suffering. By forbidding any contact with science, they condemn people to live and to die without being able to relieve their torments with tranquilizers. There may be another reason. That's why I'm so anxious to know what that dungeon conceals."

"Who lives in the castle?"

"The human chief of this planet who obeys the Rorx blindly. He bears the title of Count."

"Those despicable collaborators probably belong to the same group as Stadyr did. How vile!"

"They ought to be made an example of. There are probably many of them."

They were now close to the town and Curx could see that Setni had been right: a few wretched shacks made of mud and covered with thatch were enclosed by a thick wall. The path they were following ended at a bridge over a moat. At the other end was a heavy door flanked by two towers. Next to them was a watermill, which seemed to function normally, an indication that the fields of interference were not in constant operation.

A few gaunt, tattered peasants were digging with hoes in the fields outside the castle walls. Cattle were grazing in the sparse vegetation covering the slopes. This was a far cry from the idyllic world of the Knight of the Purple Cross. Over the roof tops loomed the imposing mass of the fortified castle; in its center was the massive tower which interested Setni.

A cart with wooden wheels, proceeding ahead of the two friends, went on the bridge. It bore a variety of vegetables. When it had reached the end, it stopped and two guards in armor gave it a cursory inspection. They then signaled to the driver to pass.

Setni and Curx soon reached the control post also. "Passes!" said one of the soldiers.

The Polluxian searched his filthy rags and opened an empty hand for the guard.

He spelled out laboriously: "Doxel and Oador, slaves for the Count for his domestic service. Is that right?"

"Yup."

"OK! Pass," said the guard, giving back the imaginary document. Don't lose it or you'll get into trouble. The count has cages full of dragons that love human flesh."

"Thank you kindly. I'll be careful," Setni muttered.

The two friends shuffled through the vaulted entrance. Setni noticed, as he went by, a *psy* mind reader. He easily neutralized it. Behind the walls was a stinking little lane where sewer water flowed down a central rut. Barefoot children covered with scabs and oozing sores played in this, splashing each other.

The two friends walked on, noting the shops in which artisans worked with primitive tools. Their technology was most elementary; there were a few gadgets, such as sheaves or pulleys, which operated normally.

Curx's compatriots had apparently adjusted to their new condition; yet all looked under-nourished and the blankness in their eyes was an indication of their hopelessness. Merchants, hucksters, water-carriers were on their way to the central square market, where purchases were concluded after interminable bargaining. Every one appeared equally poor.

Curx and Setni walked up a steep, narrow path

to the castle. Few people were there; for the most part, they were the count's servants who appeared to be treated better than others, their clothes were clean and almost new.

The second drawbridge was guarded by a dozen helmeted soldiers carrying lances and swords. Setni and Curx were looked at casually as they had been at the first check point; they had no difficulty fooling the poor simpletons. Everyone had obviously undergone the same hypnotic treatment which prevented their use of machinery, or even ancient weaponry. Everyone worked twelve hours a day and informed on any person's infraction of Rorx directives.

This time a groom was delegated to take the two visitors to the lord of the castle. He wore a livery bearing the count's coat of arms and was badly scarred by what appeared to be the marks of a whip; the Rorx used force unstintingly.

Curx hoped that his accomplice's psychic powers would dupe the count as easily as they had his slaves, or this expedition might end disastrously. They went down a maze of corridors dimly lit by torches, passed a number of inattentive sentries, then climbed a spiral staircase leading to a wooden door with heraldic motifs.

It was guarded by two sentinels. At sight of the visitors they placed the points of their halberds against their chests. Curx's heart began to beat a wild tattoo; would his companion be able to carry it off once more, or were the sentries going to unmask them?

Chapter IX

Imperturbably, Setni once more put out his empty hand. The guards then raised their halberds and opened the door. Curx began to breathe again, though the hardest part was yet to come. Preceded by the groom, the two pseudo-slaves entered a large ill-lighted room; the furnishings consisted of large wooden chests and chairs, thick animal skins and hunting trophies.

Before a large fireplace in which logs burned, a man sat with his back to the visitors. Two enormous, fierce dogs raised their heads and growled. The groom prudently stopped at a respectful distance and waited for his master to notice him. The latter turned to the newcomers, then growled:

"Why are you disturbing me, Zoff? Who are these two slaves?"

"You summoned them, my lord."

The count appeared surprised for a second, but Setni had quickly taken his measure so he muttered:

"Oh yes, Doxel and Oador. That's right, I picked them out for our Rorx rulers. Take them to the

THE ENCHANTED PLANET 139

dungeon stairs. Let them climb up, then come back to see me. Have some more logs brought in, it's freezing here." The lord of the manor sank back into his reverie, watching the flames crackling on the hearth.

The groom beckoned Setni and Curx to follow him. The servant led them to a narrow door covered by a tapestry. He opened it and stood aside to let the two slaves enter. He gave them a worried look, tinged with pity; doubtless the guests of the Rorx seldom came back down those steps.

The door slammed with finality behind the two champions. Curx began to sweat, but his companion seemed unruffled. Setni cheerfully climbed the stairs to the top of the tower. He slowed down before entering the room under the eaves. Then, suddenly making up his mind, he pushed the door open with a steady hand.

Three Rorx, perfectly motionless, were before him. Never had Curx seen his enemies so clearly. They looked like large crustaceans, with sixteen legs. Four were used for walking, the others ended in eight prehensile claws. Their carapace bore strange brownish excrescences, made viscous by mucous. Three pairs of pedunculate eyes coldly watched the intruders. Curx thought this really was their end.

But Setni had the minds of these repellent creatures under his control: they remained inert, unable to react. He went into the room and began to inspect it.

It contained many instruments with which he was unfamiliar. Some, which had screens, must have been radar systems. Setni was particularly interested in a number of curious cylinders mounted on wheels. Above them were huge glass bulbs containing electrodes; underneath them a platform housed complex circuits. A few slaves crouching on the floor were motionless. One of them was inside a cylinder. A Rorx must have been about to close its door when the two spies had come in. He was paralyzed, unable to complete his gesture.

Setni pushed the door to, locked it, then pressed a number of buttons on a control panel. The bulb lit up with a grayish light and the slave suddenly vanished. Surprised, Setni shook his head, not attempting to understand what happened; he beckoned to Curx to follow him.

They left the tower, retracing their steps but bypassing the count's room. They walked through the castle, then the town, without being challenged once. They walked in gloomy silence, depressed. A short time later, they resumed their seats in the spaceship, slammed the door and flew off. Curx, somewhat reassured, grumbled:

"Well, you scared the pants off me. I thought we were finished. Can you tell me what that diabolical dungeon contained?"

"I don't know any more than you do. Keeping the Rorx under control absorbed most of my *psy* energy, so I was unable to pick their brains. Those contraptions are used to hypnotize your people and control the planet. The cylinders were transferers. I

THE ENCHANTED PLANET 141

don't know to where they teleport the people placed inside them. How I should like to find out where they are sent. Never mind! That part isn't really important; the essential thing is that our missiles do function. We'll return to Hagen."

"I swear that we will continue to fight until the end," Curx exclaimed. "Death would be better than slavery. I only hope that you arrived in time, that our new weapons will repel those damned crustaceans."

"Who knows?" Setni replied evasively. "In any event, it would be best not to mention our little side trip. It might lower the morale of your compatriots."

"I agree. The Believers of the Last Days are poor fools, tricked by the Rorx. I'm not sorry that I had Stadyr executed."

The return trip was uneventful and the entire squadron landed in the astroport of Hagen. Olxa and Alvador were waiting for them. They knew that the "anti-missiles" had been satisfactory and they congratulated them on their success. However, before launching the last squadrons of Hagen into battle, they wanted further advice.

Curx reported on their mission. He emphasized the effectiveness of their new weapons, but he did not disguise the sad truth. According to him, hope of victory was lost; the enemies of Hagen were just too numerous. Rorx spacecraft outnumbered them ten to one. Even though one ship manned by Setni could destroy ten enemy vessels, this did not hold for the others. They could only hope for equal combat power. So this last battle would be an honorable gesture. The entire Hagen fleet would take part, but it would only delay the end.

This announcement did not appear to dismay Olxa and Alvador unduly, for they had no illusions. Only the production of amplifiers similar to the cabochon could save them, but their technicians had been unable to duplicate it.

"What do you advise us to do?" Curx asked Setni. "Should we attack at once, or shall we wait a bit longer before throwing our last forces into battle?"

"I think it would be better to delay as long as possible," Setni replied. "If you die at the head of your squadrons there will be chaos on this planet. Some of your compatriots are still hopeful. Tell them what the situation is, so they can prepare themselves. You will have done your duty and you can then leave them."

"You're right," said Olxa. "We owe them the truth. We'll telecast a message."

"May I take part in the battle?" Setni asked.

"Of course," Alvador replied. "But be careful. You must not jeopardize your chances of returning to the Galaxy."

"I haven't forgotten that I must defend my own compatriots against the Rorx. Have I enough time to get back to the transmitter before it leaves again?"

"Yes, according to our experts you have ten days."

"Perfect. I hope to annihilate quite a few of those vile crustaceans."

While the Magellanites were quickly assembling any spaceships fit for navigation, leaving Hagen only enough to patrol the approaches to the planet, Setni visited the hypogeum where the transmitter was located. The technicians had finished and the contraption was hidden in the room Setni knew. It was a pity that lack of time precluded the use of that marvelous machine to also save a few Magellanites. But sufficient energy to accomplish this would not be available for some centuries to come.

With the Rorx in Hagen, even by hibernating some citizens, stocking them with food, no human could survive for the necessary time. Even techniques of deep freezing insured human preservation for only two or three hundred years. However, the inventors knew that this machine would enable their ally to take up the struggle again. Therefore, it was a point of honor with them to show Setni all the details of its use. Upon his return to the Milky Way, he would have an almost inexhaustible source of energy to repel his adversaries.

Setni, for his part, understood what an opportunity these decent people were giving him. His cabochon enabled him to resist the hypnotic influence of Archimago and Duessa. But from now on, his powers would be magnified a hundredfold and he would be able to protect the people of the Milky Way.

But the situation was paradoxical: all these unfortunates had actually died long ago! Only their distant descendants were still living under the yoke of the cruel Rorx. The Knight of the Purple Cross and his peers were Magellanites: they did not know that their ancestors had died happy and free, at a time when the Rorx had not yet conquered the Large Magellanic Cloud. Unfortunately, the transmitter which had been invented by their own people would not serve to free them. Only the people of the Milky Way would benefit from it, because once Setni had demonstrated his enormous strength by throwing Archimago and Duessa out of his galaxy, the Rorx would think twice before attacking.

A few days after the raid, Curx told Setni the fleet was ready. The Magellanites had collected two thousand ships of all sizes. The Rorx had twenty thousand at their disposal. In recognition of his services rendered, Setni was given command of one of the four squadrons.

They were to be arranged in the shape of a diamond. Alvador was at the head, Curx and Olxa at the two sides, while Setni brought up the rear. The formation created an illusion of enormous power. Setni had seldom seen so many ships assembled. But they were nothing compared to the Rorx, as the astronaut soon found out.

The enemy awaited them at one day's flight from Hagen. Their legions stretched to the horizon; they intended to swallow up their puny, foolhardy challengers. The Rorx obviously had not yet learned about Setni and Curx's expedition behind their lines.

The enemy forces were deployed in a crescent shape, to close in on their adversaries in a pincer movement, cutting off any possible retreat. Serpents of flame were soon licking Alvador's spaceships. The riposte was instantaneous: many tapered missiles were shot at the Rorx ships. At first, they disregarded them, thinking they would be easy to eliminate; but when the first fires broke out in the midst of the Rorx formations, panic began among the survivors.

For the first time since the beginning of their war, the hideous crustaceans had to flee. Alvador pressed his advantage to rush into the midst of the enemy squadrons. His weapons scored bull's-eyes every time. The enemy loss was enormous. But the Rorx forces were too numerous. As they fled, they fired back furiously; countless Magellanite ships were put out of commission.

It was then that Curx and Olxa came to the rescue. This time, the enemy wings folded under the attack of missiles protected by selenium armor. The explosion of anti-matter warheads destroyed everything within a vast sector; for every ship put out of commission, ten more rushed in.

It was at this point that Setni decided to enter the melee, for the Rorx appeared to still be intent on encircling the Magellanite squadrons. Fortunately, the density of enemy spaceships was less in this sector. This enabled Setni to husband his missiles by making use of his *psy* powers to destroy his foes; he was remarkably successful. It seemed clear that if the Magellanites had been equipped with cabochons, they would have defeated their enemies despite their numerical inferiority. However, such was not the case; the balance began to tip toward the Rorx.

All the units under the command of Alvador were now engaged in close combat. When a Magellanite commander ran out of missiles, he would rush the enemy ships. In this manner he could destroy one more enemy ship as the Rorx, overwhelmed on all sides, could not watch every opponent.

Setni managed, until the end, to keep open a narrow lane through which several surviving squadrons could flee. He was the last to leave; thanks to his reserve of missiles, he was able to discourage his pursuers.

In this way, twenty-four spaceships returned to the astroport of Hagen. Curx's and Olxa's were among them, but Alvador had been killed in battle. However, this unexpected development had given the Rorx pause; they did not pursue their advantage. They withdrew to some distance from Hagen to lick their wounds and meditate on the danger of the new weapons. Fearing a renewed assault by Magellanite reserves, they awaited the arrival of reinforcements before resuming their offensive.

This unhoped for respite was used in an unexpected manner by Curx and Olxa. They decided to get married before dying together in battle.

Setni was present at the simple ceremony, tears in his eyes at the injustice of their fate. After the wedding, he went to see his two friends in the control tower of the astroport, which was one of the few safe places left in Hagen.

The city was now in a state of upheaval. Panic-stricken as a result of Alvador's announcement, people had fled to neighboring hills, taking food and clothing with them. They hoped to escape the Rorx by hiding in caverns. Gangs of looters roamed the city, stealing, killing, setting fires. There were scenes of orgy everywhere. Little remained of the former Magellanite way of life.

The couple viewed with sadness the smoke rising from the alabaster towers of Hagen. Setni respected their silence. Then Curx gave him a long look, as though seeing him for the first time.

"Well, this is the end of Hagen. Our descendants shall live as slaves. Your coming had given me hope, but we were doomed. You will soon be back in your own country and my consolation is knowing you will keep up the fight, thanks to our transferer. Please don't forget our descendants; if you can help them, please do, in memory of what we have given you."

"I won't forget, you can be sure. I've seen the Rorx cruelty. If it is ever within my power to avenge you, I swear they'll pay one hundred times over. Tell me, what are your immediate plans?"

Curx looked at Olxa questioningly, as though the decision was hers. "We haven't much choice, dear friend. There are not enough of our ships to repulse the Rorx, and we have no desire to be slaves. Curx has told me what you saw on the planet you visited. Not one of us will accept such an ignoble fate, nor have we any desire to become counts. We'll just wait for the final onslaught. We still have a few ships fit for flight. We shall die, but we'll sell our lives dearly.

"As for you," Curx then said, "don't delay in taking off via the transferer. You must seal the door of the chamber it now occupies, so that the Rorx will never discover it. And now, if you don't mind, we'll say good-bye to you, so that we can take advantage of the few hours remaining to us. Just think, how stupid we are: Olxa and I have been in love for years but all we thought about was impressing each other. This disaster has helped us overcome our crazy pride. We thank you from the bottom of our hearts for everything you did for us. Good-bye, Setni!"

Olxa lightly kissed Setni on the cheek, smiled and left, her hand holding Curx's tightly. They vanished down an anti-gravity well and he remained alone.

Setni sat in front of one of the vast bays dominating the astroport. He had a splendid view of Hagen which still looked intact. The automatic services that continued air-conditioning and cleaning were still functioning. All the citizens had fled, in fear of a Rorx bombardment.

"Why bother to continue the struggle?" the Polluxian thought sadly. I am only a pawn on a gigantic chessboard, an infinitely small man pushed around by immeasurably powerful forces. Fate declared that the Magellanites would build a transferer, in the hope of saving a few representatives of their race. As it turned out, the transferer enabled an inhabitant of the Milky Way to save his own people, by using a psychic weapon powerful enough to repulse spies the Rorx had sent into the Milky Way. The Psyborgs knew what they were doing when they sent a human to a planet which had unexpectedly appeared from the cosmos, but what did he represent for them? Probably nothing important. What a debt the Confederation had contracted! But would they ever know about what had transpired? The fact that one of their people had been projected to so distant a past would seem incredible to them. He must return to the planet of the Knight of the Purple Cross, so as to complete the task entrusted to him by the Psyborgs. He had to escape from the Rorx so that the transferer could send him back to his starting point.

Setni scanned the screens flickering about him: they showed a gigantic fleet massed near Hagen. The Rorx were going to mount their final assault soon. He must leave the astroport and take refuge in the transferer before the arrival of the invaders.

Yet the Polluxian could not leave; he wanted to be present at Hagen's end. He stayed another day, watching the screens and the dead city, eating food from the automatic distributors.

At last he saw the Rorx Armada, like a gigantic bird of prey, diving toward Hagen. A few ships took off, aiming straight at the squadrons of destruction, preferring death to captivity.

There were voices from loud speakers: Olxa and Curx bidding him a last good-bye. "Perhaps you can still hear me, Setni. We want you to know we have no regrets," Olxa said. "Men are born free, with equal rights. Henceforth our compatriots will live in odious tyranny. Only death will enable us to safeguard our freedom."

"Don't forget, my friend, that our sacrifice must not be in vain," Curx added. "Thanks to us, you will have a weapon that will enable your compatriots to avoid our wretched fate. If you have not already done so, leave Hagen quickly and take shelter in the blockhouse which houses the transmitter. The enemy cannot harm you there."

The message ended there.

The Polluxian looked for another moment at the minute radar spots aiming straight at the Rorx ships. He saw one more small spot on the edge of the evil crescent. It made some progress, for a moment, toward the center of an enemy grouping, then it disappeared. The last astronauts of Hagen had been defeated.

Thoroughly downcast, Setni left the control tower. The anti-gravitational well took him to the underground. He followed the secret tunnel leading to the transferer, riding along on the conveyor belt which spiraled down to the depths. He went through fortified gates and set the destruction switches which would bury the machine under tons of rock, to protect it against the damages of time and eventual search by the Rorx.

Setni then was alone in the hypogeum he had uncovered such a short time ago. Little did he dream then that he would be its last visitor. He sat down in the majestic chair, pensively contemplating the lights dancing about in the machines.

He still had to make psychic contact with the memory bank of the giant computer; he gave the order to transmit to Unia's parents the legend of the magic mirror, so that they could warn her about it when, in the distant future, he would liberate them from the dragon. Then Setni fed it the image of the magic object and the place where it was to be hidden, at the moment when he would reach the planet of Archimago and Duessa. Now he waited calmly, in complete silence, for the wave that would come from the depths of space to take him back to his point of departure.

Suddenly his brain felt a kind of undertow. The luminescent plasma filaments wound about him, gripping his mind. Despite his anxiety, he marvelled that instantly, a faithful copy of each of his molecules would be transmitted through space. Different atoms would be assembled to duplicate his body elsewhere. Then he sank into the void.

Setni's first thought was to wonder anxiously if the Magellanites' machine had functioned properly, if he had been returned to his point of departure.

Nothing around him seemed to have changed. He could move his arms and legs, the cabochon sparkled on his belt. He got up and stretched, as if after a long sleep. Diamond dust flitted about like fireflies in the machines around him.

His well-conditioned mind delved into the past, to draw from energy accumulated during eons of time, atoms scattered in the heart of the Magellanic

Clouds. He reassembled them into two familiar shapes: Olxa and Curx. They stood before him, raising their hands in a friendly gesture and smiled. Comforted by their fleeting presence, he allowed the beloved figures to fade and dissolve.

Setni left the room to which the transferer had borne him, and strode through the hypogeum where the statues of dead Magellanites gazed down on him. He found his armor, which he put on again, and had himself teleported to the stop of the old anti-G well through which he had come. He took one last melancholy look at the remains of glorious Hagen.

A desire for revenge welled up inside the Polluxian. He materialized before the camp pitched in front of the city. He knew now what must be done.

The knight who was standing guard recognized him instantly and heralded his return. The Knight of the Purple Cross rushed out to welcome him. Setni responded to the brotherly hug as the knight said, with some concern:

"You were not gone very long, dear friend. Did you find out the secret?"

"Yes! Now I know about the origins of your race. This marvelous city was built long ago by your ancestors, who were then powerful and free. They were attacked by the Rorx and, despite their advance technology, reduced to slavery. Any scientific or psychic research was forbidden; these fiends took on the shapes of Archimago and Duessa to hoodwink you."

"I'd always suspected this tragedy," said Purple

Cross sadly. "So, our masters are named Rorx and have been our oppressors for millenia. How sad. Is there no hope that we may some day regain our freedom?"

"Perhaps. Those fiends, after conquering your country, the Large Magellanic Cloud—a galaxy far from our Milky Way—sent agents among us to find out if we could put up much resistance. I think I can teach them a lesson and also prevent them from sending your planet back to the Magellanic Clouds. Some day, my compatriots will be able to free your people, but they still have a lot to learn before catching up with Rorx expertise. I'll do everything I can to keep you from your tormentors. Dear friend, I'll fight like hell, but alone. If there is anything I can do for you, tell me what it is. I owe your ancestors a debt which I've sworn never to forget."

"Well spoken, noble friend. Your loyalty warms my heart. I know you will always defend the oppressed, wherever they may be: therefore I shall not plead for my wretched people. But send me back to the woman I love."

"So be it. You will know that I shall never forget you, that I'll fight the Rorx to the finish. Farewell, Knight of the Purple Cross. May you live happily with the gentle Unia. The woman I love can never belong to me."

Concentrating hard, Setni then teleported the worthy knight to the castle where Unia and her parents awaited him. He took a moment to observe

Unia's joy, then tore himself away and returned to the enchanted isle.

There he took one last look at the ruins of Hagen beneath the lake, dematerialized the magic knights whose services he no longer required, then waited confidently for the arrival of Archimago and Duessa. The confrontation was about to take place. If he won, the Milky Way would be safe, at least for a while.

If he did not, his compatriots would suffer the fate of the Magellanites. Centuries of pain and servitude would then be their lot.

Epilogue

Setni did not have long to wait: the two Rorx were determined to deal with their foe. They showed up in their real shapes. They did not realize that the telepathic and telekinetic powers of their adversary were a hundred times stronger, since he had possessed the Hagen transferer. He was no longer a helpless puppet.

He cast a circle of fire around the two evil creatures, which they tried to repel as flames singed their carapaces. They riposted by trying to cause a cloudburst, but they were fighting a superior foe.

Setni summoned a gale to blow away the dark clouds. Cornered, the two Rorx flew up in the shape of winged dragons and fled as fast as they were able. Setni changed himself into an armored monster spitting fire; he clawed them as he broiled them alive. Hideous howls filled the air. Beneath them, terrified humans hid in their houses, believing the end of the world had come.

Setni did not want to kill the Rorx; he wanted to teach them to be panic stricken at the thought of confronting inhabitants of the Milky Way. He conjured up a whirlwind, dashing the two dragons to the ground. Archimago and Duessa found themselves chained in a dark cell, much like the ones where they had once imprisoned Setni.

He made them believe they were surrounded by hideous demons that dug sharp prongs into them, piercing their carapaces and drawing a viscous fluid. The prisoners, dying a thousand deaths, tried vainly to repulse their tormentors. At last they were experiencing the suffering they had for centuries inflicted on the unfortunate Magellanites. When Setni decided the punishment was sufficient, he changed pace.

This time a frightening ghost, like Error, came to torment the hellish pair, filling them with panic. The Rorx twisted about helplessly, trying to avoid the black coils of the nauseous monster. He filled them with paralyzing anguish; then, when they had lost all hope, he summoned them before a tribunal of Magellanites. The latter, in a lengthy indictment, read out the list of tribulations they had suffered since their people had been enslaved by the Rorx.

The sentence was immediately carried out. The two prisoners were shut up in a magic sphere which would take them back to the Large Magellanic Cloud. This was final proof of the supremacy of a single human being over the presumptuous creatures who had tried to capture the Milky Way.

So Archimago and Duessa left the Galaxy which they had thought to conquer. They were in a pitiful state when their peers picked them up, shivering with terror.

THE ENCHANTED PLANET

Setni had fulfilled his mission, there was nothing further to keep him on this planet. He now had to report on his mission to the Psyborgs. He did not have long to wait. A space ship came to pick him up at once, bringing him to the powerful trinity who had saved humankind. Wotan, Oberon and the noble Dahut were sitting on their crystal thrones in all their majesty, when he appeared.

"Congratulations, little man," Wotan rumbled in his deep voice. "You managed to outmaneuver those who, arrogantly, thought they could enslave your compatriots. Your race has been saved, at least, for the time being."

"You are entitled to a reward commensurate with your achievement, brave Polluxian," said Oberon. "Make a wish; it will be granted."

"I ask nothing for myself, although my heart yearns to finish my days with Nicolette. The plight of the Magellanites has saddened me, so I ask that the planet of the Knight of the Purple Cross not return to the Magellanic Clouds. That worthy knight deserves to live happy and free with Unia. Can you grant this?"

"Yes," Dahut said. "We shall send their planet to a distant constellation, at the edge of the Milky Way, where your compatriots have not yet been. There, your friends can live like human beings."

"Many thanks. Nothing could give me greater pleasure. In this way, I can repay their ancestors."

"Don't be too grateful, my friend," Wotan interrupted. "We should like to do more for you. Unfortunately, we have had to make other decisions about your fate. You have been trained to use extraordinary powers which will one day belong to all humans. Unfortunately it is impossible now to allow you to enjoy your talent for teleportation and telepathy. You would be tempted to gain too much power over your peers. Humans are not yet ready for total psychic power. Such changes must be gradual. You and your compatriots have not finished with the Rorx. We shall always be ready to come to your assistance. The Polluxians, in the future, will have to repel a more powerful invasion than this one. The fear that those evil creatures feel will not last forever. So, once more, you will have to forget your adventures. You will report that the space ship you saw was only an ovoid asteroid, made of titanium and iron. The Great Brains will probably suspect some mystery, but they will never find the truth. Your brain will retain no recollection of the battle you fought. Nicolette, you know, is only an Elf, a phantasm from our fairyland; you cannot take her back to Kalapol. You will have to forget her also. Oblivion will serve as a bandage for your wounded spirit. Good-bye, Setni."

The Psyborg Trinity vanished at once, before Setni had time to reply.

"Son of a gun!" exclaimed Pentoser, as he saw his friend crawling out of the air lock of the *Zineb*. "Back so soon? What did you find in that wreck?"

"Absolutely nothing. For a very good reason; it's only an ovoid asteroid. Just a block of stone that has been travelling in space."

THE ENCHANTED PLANET

"Is that so! It's hard to believe. I could have sworn. . . . Didn't you mention an air lock?" Pentoser asked.

"Oh, I believe you," the astronaut said, shrugging his shoulders. "Hell! We're going to look like damn fools."

"Leave it to me," Setni assured him.

From the control room of the space ship he grabbed a mike and sent the following message:

"Captain Setni reporting. False alarm. I examined the unidentified object on all sides. It's nothing but an ovoid meteor. We're returning to Kalapol. End of message."

Far away, from the edge of the Milky Way, the Knight of the Purple Cross and Unia looked wonderingly up at the new constellations shimmering in the firmament. They both wondered on which of those shiny points lived the man who had saved them from Rorx oppression. They yearned to see him again some day. Little did they realize that their fairyland prince had forgotten them, forever.

DAW sf BOOKS

Presenting the international science fiction spectrum:

- ☐ **GAMES PSYBORGS PLAY** by Pierre Barbet. They made a whole world their arena and a whole race their pawns. (#UQ1087—95¢)

- ☐ **THE OVERLORDS OF WAR** by Gerard Klein. Translated by John Brunner, this is a masterpiece of advanced cosmic conception. (#UQ1099—95¢)

- ☐ **STARMASTERS' GAMBIT** by Gerard Klein. Games players of the cosmos—an interstellar adventure equal to the best. (#UQ1068—95¢)

- ☐ **THE ORCHID CAGE** by Herbert W. Franke. The problem of robots and intelligence as confronted by Germany's master of hard-core science fiction. (#UQ1082—95¢)

- ☐ **BAPHOMET'S METEOR** by Pierre Barbet. A startling counter-history of atomic Crusaders and an alternate world. (#UQ1035—95¢)

- ☐ **2018 A.D. OR THE KING KONG BLUES** by Sam J. Lundwall. A shocker in the tradition of *A Clockwork Orange*. (#UY1161—$1.25)

- ☐ **HARD TO BE A GOD** by A. & B. Strugatski. A brilliant novel of advanced men on a backward planet—by Russia's most outstanding sf writers. (#UY1141—$1.25)

- ☐ **THE MIND NET** by Herbert W. Franke. Their starship was kidnapped by an alien brain from a long-dead world. (#UQ1136—95¢)

DAW BOOKS are represented by the publishers of Signet and Mentor Books, THE NEW AMERICAN LIBRARY, INC.

THE NEW AMERICAN LIBRARY, INC.,
P.O. Box 999, Bergenfield, New Jersey 07621

Please send me the DAW BOOKS I have checked above. I am enclosing $_____(check or money order—no currency or C.O.D.'s). Please include the list price plus 25¢ a copy to cover mailing costs.

Name_____

Address_____

City_____State_____Zip Code_____

Please allow at least 3 weeks for delivery